Double Dare and Other Stories

The past, the present and the future are cleverly woven into individual stories about four children living in a city. They are from very different backgrounds but each experiences an adventure of a very special kind in which his or her innermost dreams are revealed.

Lorraine has always wanted her own pet, but what is the secret of the silkworms she finds in a box? Charlie adores going 'Over-the-Log' but is amazed to discover another world, far removed from his own life. Terry has neither mother, nor family and lives in a Children's Home. Little does he guess how far-reaching the consequences of his Double Dare will be. Maggie befriends old Mr. Winterbourne and realises she must somehow find the soldier who haunts him from the past.

Here are four spell-binding stories, each with a hint of the supernatural and a fascinating glimpse into unknown places, yet always within the familiar background of home and friends. The children could live next door, but the adventures they have, and the friends they make, are literally out of this world . . .

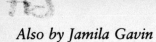

Also by Jamila Gavin

I Want to be an Angel
Kamla and Kate
Kamla and Kate Again

for older readers

The Singing Bowls

JAMILA GAVIN

Double Dare
and other Stories

Illustrated by Simon Willby

MAMMOTH

To Indra and Rohan

First published in Great Britain 1982
by Methuen Children's Books Ltd
Published 1992 by Mammoth
an imprint of Mandarin Paperbacks
Michelin House, 81 Fulham Road, London SW3 6RB

Mandarin is an imprint of the Octopus Publishing Group,
a division of Reed International Books Ltd

Text copyright © 1982 Jamila Gavin
Illustrations copyright © 1982 Methuen Children's Books Ltd

ISBN 0 7497 0959 6

A CIP catalogue record for this title
is available from the British Library

Printed in Great Britain
by Cox & Wyman Ltd, Reading, Berkshire

Contents

1 The Mulberry Tree

'Why can't I have a pet?' wailed Lorraine for the fifty millionth time.

'Can't you stop asking, girl?' sighed her mother wearily. 'You know we're not allowed pets in these flats.'

'Old Mrs. Petrovitch has a cat – how come she's allowed?' persisted Lorraine.

'She's not allowed,' snapped Mum. 'No one knows about it, at least no one from the council does. We can't help knowing – the smell is terrible.'

'No one would know if I had a tortoise or a gold fish. Why can't I have one of those?'

'Because I say no! You can't even keep your own bed tidy let alone look after a tortoise. It would just be more work for me. They have to be kept clean and fed, just like anything else,' replied Mum firmly.

'But Mum . . .'

Lorraine's father rustled his newspaper impatiently and glared at Lorraine. 'Drop it now, will you?' he ordered.

'But Dad . . .'

'I said DROP IT!' roared Dad, ferocious as a lion.

Lorraine burst into tears. Dad slammed down his newspaper. 'I'm off to work,' he said. 'Can't stand this racket. Bye now, love.' He gave his wife a quick peck on the cheek, and went out, slamming the front door.

'Now you've gone and upset your Dad,' exclaimed Mum angrily.

Lorraine howled even louder, noisily rubbing her eyes and nose into her sleeve. For a moment Mum stood looking as if she were going to shake the living daylights out of her, then changed her mind. She put an arm round Lorraine instead and led her over to the small, narrow balcony overlooking the city.

'Look, honey! Here we are, eleven floors up into the sky. Even the sparrows don't fly up here. We have no garden, nothing. It would be cruel to keep a pet up here. Even a tortoise needs grass to crawl through. It would be no life for him at the top of a tower block.'

'Then ... w ... why can't I have a goldfish?' hiccoughed Lorraine.

'Goldfish need cleaning out, too, and you won't do it!' argued Mum. 'Besides, how would you like to swim round and round a bowl by yourself for ever?'

Lorraine sniffed. Her mother led her back to the table. 'Come on now, finish your breakfast. You'll be late for school and I'll be late for work.'

Lorraine and her mother walked to school in silence. Lorraine still hiccoughed from time to time and Mum made her blow her nose.

As they neared school, Lorraine said, 'Nearly every kid in school has a pet. Leroy Martin, his Dad's got a pet alligator. They keep it in the bath.'

'What!' shrieked Mum in disgust.

'Leroy says it's getting a bit big for the bath now and they'll have to get rid of it.'

'Where'll they do that? asked Mum.

'I dunno. Perhaps they'll drop it over into the canal.'

'We'd better warn Dad next time he goes fishing,' laughed Mum.

'Then they're thinking of getting a snake,' continued Lorraine.

'Ugh!' exclaimed Mum.

They reached the school gates. Mum kissed

Lorraine goodbye and waved all the way till she was inside. She gave a sigh as she walked away. If only Lorraine would stop going on about pets.

But Lorraine couldn't stop thinking about pets. She daydreamed all the time, even in class. She imagined having a pet monkey which sat on her shoulder, or a long, glittery snake which wound round her neck and terrified everyone. Her favourite daydream was to be like the beautiful princess she saw once in a book, who held two gold and black spotted cheetahs on the ends of long, gold chains. Imagine! What a sight she'd make, walking two cheetahs in the park.

But the nearest Lorraine had ever come to owning a pet was when Micky Macgonagle gave her a little white mouse. He passed it to her in class one day and said she could keep it.

'I love you, Micky Macgonagle. I shall marry you when I grow up,' she had sighed.

'You don't have to do that,' said Micky, screwing up his face with disgust. 'I'll take it back.'

But Lorraine had already popped the mouse

into her pocket and kept her hand protectively over the small, quivering animal.

When she got home, the mouse wasn't there! Frantically she shook out her anorak, her cardigan, her skirt, and even her knickers, but there was no sign of it.

'What are you up to?' Mum asked suspiciously.

'Micky Macgonagle gave me a pet mouse to KEEP!' Lorraine wailed, grief-stricken. 'But it's gone! It was in my pocket . . .'

Mum shrieked and jumped on the sofa.

'What the dickens is going on?' demanded Dad, who had just come home.

'I've lost my pet mouse,' sobbed Lorraine.

'Find it! Find it!' squealed Mum. 'Get it out of here.'

But though they searched the flat from top to bottom, they never saw it. Lorraine got a smack and was sent to bed.

'The rule is NO PETS, and that goes for mice too, so don't you dare bring any creatures up here again,' threatened Mum.

'DON'T YOU DARE!' said Dad, to underline the point.

*   *   *

The next day was Saturday. Lorraine peered down through the balcony, idly watching a bunch of kids far, far below her. They looked like ants as they scurried this way and that. They were kicking something, a cardboard box perhaps.

'Can I go out to play, Mum?' Lorraine called.

'Yes, but remember you'll have to use the stairs. The lift's broke again!'

Lorraine ran down each flight which had twelve steps to every landing. She ran down six, then jumped six; whirled round the corner, ran down six, then jumped six . . . She did this twenty two times! It was the quickest way down without the lift.

By the time she reached the bottom the kids had abandoned the cardboard box and were chasing each other about. Lorraine noticed the box was bound by a rubber band. Curiously she bent down and picked it up.

It was dark inside the cardboard box. Just a few specks of lights glinted like stars where someone had pierced holes for air. The little creatures wriggled over each other, nibbling at leaves which lined the box. Their heads moved up and down as they gnawed and munched.

Suddenly the lid was pulled off. They were

thrown from darkness to light, but still the little creatures never stopped nibbling.

Lorraine stared at them, spellbound.

'What are they?' The children crowded round. Someone said, 'They're caterpillars.'

'No, they're silkworms,' said another. 'I've got some at school.'

'I'm going to keep them,' said Lorraine. 'I'll go and put some lettuce leaves in the box. They've almost finished these leaves.'

'Lettuce won't do,' said the child who seemed to know. 'Silkworms only eat mulberry leaves.'

'Where do I find mulberry leaves?' asked Lorraine. But the child had picked up his bike and cycled off. 'Perhaps Dad will know,' she thought.

On Saturday Dad always helped his brother-in-law on the vegetable stall in the market. There was a big queue of people at the stall. Many of them were Lorraine's neighbours. They came to Dad's stall because he sold the sort of fruit and vegetables you could not buy in the shops along the High Street such as yams, papayas, cassavas and mangoes; lady's fingers, chillies and mountains of peanuts!

Lorraine wriggled her way through the legs and shopping bags until she reached her father.

'Where do I find mulberry leaves, Dad?' she called up to him.

Dad was weighing a great bunch of large, green West Indian bananas. 'I don't know, Lorraine,' he said impatiently. 'There ain't no such fancy trees round here. Why?'

'I need them for my silkworms,' she said, opening the box for him to see. When she saw her father's horrified face she crammed the lid back on and began to crawl back through the shoppers.

'Don't you go taking them creatures back home, do you hear?' he called after her. 'Your Mum will go mad! She can't stand creepy-crawlies!'

'They're not creepy-crawlies,' muttered Lorraine; 'they're silkworms and they're mine.'

'Hi there!' called a voice behind her. 'What you got there, little lady?'

It was her grown-up cousin, Franklyn. Lorraine opened the box and said proudly, 'They're my pets!'

'Caterpillars!' exclaimed Franklyn.

'Silkworms,' corrected Lorraine firmly, 'but they only eat mulberry leaves. The ones in the box are almost finished so I must find a mulberry tree soon or they will die. Dad says that's a fancy tree not found round here. What shall I do?'

'Well, there's some fancy trees on my bus route,' said Franklyn. 'Come for a ride with me, and when we come to the houses up the hill – the big ones with gardens all round – perhaps someone will tell you if there is a mulberry tree to be found.'

Lorraine sat on the bus, carefully holding the cardboard box on her lap. Franklyn shut the doors and started up the engine. They were off!

Lorraine looked out of the window, wondering what a mulberry tree looked like. The bus moved up the High Street past rows and rows of shops, and streets and streets of terraced houses with tiny gardens in front. Most had low walls or dusty hedges; sometimes there was a grimy hydrangea bush or a thin row of marigolds – but no trees.

They passed her own block of flats and on past the vast, wind-swept playing fields. Then the bus began to climb the hill.

Suddenly, Lorraine noticed how wide the road had become, and it was lined with flowering cherry trees which swirled like a snow storm every time the wind blew.

Then she saw the houses; not in tight rows with hardly a centimetre between them, but each like a castle with great gardens all around.

The gardens were like parks with lots of trees; some which gracefully drooped their blossoms over the wall, and others which spread their shade like green pools. Some trees were taller than the houses and stood like sentries on guard duty, while others were only just high enough to nod and scratch at the downstairs windows.

Lorraine bobbed up and down from one side of the bus to the other. 'Franklyn, what does a mulberry tree look like?'

A lady got up and rang the bell. 'If you're looking for a mulberry tree, I think there's one just a few doors along from me,' she said kindly. 'Come with me and I'll show you.'

Lorraine followed the lady off the bus. Franklyn's bus had almost reached the end of the line and would soon be turning round to come back on the return journey. 'I'll give you a toot when I get here,' he said.

Lorraine and the lady walked past one or two very grand houses, trim, well-painted and proud, then they stopped outside a very old gate. With its peeling paint and rusty drainpipes, the huge, dark-brick house looked lonely and uncared for, almost hidden from view by the garden which had grown up like a jungle.

'That is a mulberry tree,' said the lady, pointing to a broad, leafy tree. Then she waved goodbye and went on her way.

The mulberry tree stood by some large bay windows at the front of the house. The afternoon sun glinted through the rich, green broad-veined leaves like flashes of gold.

Lorraine stood staring at it from the gate, wondering what to do. She felt a little bit frightened. Did she dare walk up the path and pull off some of the leaves? The branches hung low, dipping their leaves into the long overgrown grass. The path had almost disappeared, and brambles and weeds entangled the house.

Suddenly, through a gap in the branches of the mulberry tree, Lorraine saw a face at the bay window. It was the face of an old lady and she was waving and smiling.

Lorraine waved back. The face went away, and then a few moments later the door opened and the old lady's head appeared, just visible above the weeds.

'Hello, my dear!' she called to Lorraine. 'It's nice to see a child round here. There aren't many you know – they're all old people like me!'

'I've got some silk-worms in this box,' said Lorraine boldly. 'They need some mulberry leaves to eat or they'll die. Can I pick some off your tree?'

The old lady made her way slowly down the path to have a look. 'Aren't they pretty creatures,' she said happily. 'Of course they need mulberry leaves. Come and pick as many as you like.'

Lorraine waded through the grass to the tree and began to pick the oval-shaped leaves. As the silkworms began to nibble once more, the old lady watched them intently, and quietly whispered;

'Nibble, nibble, hungry lady,
Eat through the dark green leaves.
Though you munch your own green home,
Think what households you'll enrich.'

Then she sighed. 'I haven't seen silkworms since I left China many years ago! Did you know that silkworms were first discovered in China?'

'I don't know much about silkworms,' said Lorraine.

'Well,' the old lady continued, 'many, many years ago – or so the story goes – a princess was walking in her garden when she suddenly noticed a silkworm spinning its cocoon. She discovered that the cocoon was being spun from one long, fine, silvery thread.

'After this discovery, the Chinese learnt how to gather these threads and weave them into one of the most beautiful and treasured materials in the world – silk! From then on, all Chinese emperors and very rich people wore magnificent clothes made from silk.

'The rest of the world was amazed and wanted to know how the silk was made and where it came from, but the Chinese refused to give away the secret. Anyone who did would be killed immediately.

'The secret was kept for hundreds of years, until, one day, a Chinese princess was to be married to an Indian prince. To show her love for him she hid some silkworm eggs and seeds from the mulberry tree in her hair, and smuggled them out of China.

'At last! The secret of silk was out! And now they make silk all round the world, even here!'

Lorraine looked in amazement at her box of wriggling silkworms. Perhaps now her Mum would let her keep them. 'Can these spin silk?'

'Of course they can,' replied the old lady. 'They spin their cocoon with a silken thread,

but if you were to collect that thread it would mean unwinding the cocoon and the silkworm would die.'

'I couldn't do that!' gasped Lorraine.

'If you leave the cocoon, you will see another miracle. The little silkworm will live hidden inside the cocoon for about ten days, then he will work his way out, not as an earth-bound worm but transformed into a beautiful silkmoth with gossamer wings. He will fly about and live gloriously for just a day or two, then die.'

'Oh!' sighed Lorraine sadly.

'Now, how are we going to make sure that these little creatures will get enough to eat? Are there no mulberry trees near where you live?' asked the old lady.

Lorraine shook her head sadly. Then suddenly she had an idea. 'Could you look after them for me? We live in a council flat and we aren't allowed to keep pets. Anyway, my Mum hates creepy crawlies.'

The old lady took the box gently from Lorraine. 'Yes,' she said, 'I'll look after them for you, but only if you promise to come and see me often.'

Lorraine promised. A bus stopped beyond the gate and the horn beeped. It was Franklyn. 'Did you find what you wanted?' he asked.

Lorraine said goodbye to the old lady and skipped happily to the bus.

'Yes,' she told Franklyn. 'I found what I wanted.'

At last Lorraine could say she had a pet! And not just one pet, but eight!

'My pets start off as one thing and change into another!' she announced triumphantly at school. 'And they make rich clothes for kings and queens!'

'You can't cuddle them though,' said Marlene Banks.

'And you can't take them for walks,' said Sean Daly.

'Who cares?' retorted Lorraine. 'These are special.'

The next time Lorraine went up the hill in Franklin's bus to see the old lady, she was invited in for orange squash and biscuits. Franklin said he would toot for her as usual on the way back.

Lorraine followed the old lady into the dark, dark inside of the house. She shivered, for although the sun was shining quite strongly outside, its warmth did not seem able to penetrate the thick, brick walls of the house or the leafy screen the mulberry tree made across the bay windows.

Standing in the gloomy hall, she noticed that in whichever corner she looked, or on whatever wall, there was something interesting to see. There were strange pictures, odd-shaped ornaments, long, twisty pipes and terrifying, wooden masks; there were stuffed birds in glass jars, antlers over a doorway and a huge tiger skin with its head and spiky, white teeth grinning up at her from the floor. It was like being in a church, a zoo and a junk shop all rolled into one.

'My husband's job took him all over the world,' said the old lady, when she noticed Lorraine looking round in amazement. 'All I have left now are the things we collected together; he's been dead for nearly ten years.'

She shuffled down a long corridor and opened another door. Lorraine, who had followed close behind, decided this must be the living room. It seemed warmer than the rest of the house, and lighter. A gas fire was burning in the grate of an enormous old-fashioned fireplace and a large, cushiony sofa was pulled up close by. This room, too, was crammed with objects covering every flat surface to be found – tables, window ledges, the top of a piano and the mantlepiece.

'Where are my silkworms?' asked Lorraine.

'In the conservatory,' came the reply.

There were some tall windows that went from the ceiling to the floor at the far end of the room. The old lady undid the catches, pushed open two windows which turned out to be doors, and they went through into a large glass house.

It was the first time that Lorraine felt really warm. The conservatory was hot and steamy like a jungle, smelling of tomatoes and geraniums.

The box of silkworms was on a sunny ledge. Lorraine put her little finger inside and let the fat, white, roly-poly bodies wriggle over it.

The old lady said, 'I've been collecting some twigs to put in the box. The silkworms will need them for support when they start spinning their cocoons.'

Lorraine placed the twigs carefully among the mulberry leaves, then they went out to the front to pick more leaves.

And so Lorraine and the old lady became friends. The old lady was always glad to see Lorraine. Her face was often at the window, peering through the mulberry tree, waiting for Lorraine to come skipping up the path, and she always had a special treat ready for her like home-made chocolate cake or iced biscuits.

In return, Lorraine sometimes brought the

old lady something from her father's stall, like a bag of lady's fingers or a bunch of bananas. Best of all was the day when Lorraine brought her a large, rosy mango. The old lady was thrilled.

'Oh, how I love mangoes! When I was in Africa, I almost lived on mangoes. It was so hot, I used to sit and eat them in a cool bath – that was the best way. Then you could suck them to your heart's content and not worry about getting the juice all over your clothes!'

Lorraine laughed. 'I'll have to try that,' she said happily.

Then the day came when the silkworms began to spin their cocoons. The old lady was watching as usual at the window, longing for Lorraine to come so that she could show her the silkworms, their heads tossing to and fro as they began to wind the threads round the twigs and round their own bodies.

But Lorraine did not come that day – nor the next. The days went by, and still she did not come.

Once, when the old lady was waiting as usual at her window, she saw the bus go past on up the hill. She thought she would try and get to the gate and wave it down when it had turned round and was on its way back. But by the time she had taken off her bedroom slippers and got into her shoes – her old fingers stumbling over the buckles – by the time she had opened the front door and started to hobble down the garden path, the bus had swept past without even slowing down.

'Oh dear!' she sighed. 'I wish Lorraine would come. She will miss seeing how the silk worms spin their cocoons.'

Lorraine was lying in a warm, dark, silken bed. She wanted to wriggle out, but her body felt helpless and trapped.

The early morning sun fell across her bed. Deep, deep inside, Lorraine felt she wanted to throw the covers off and break out.

She began to push and struggle, but her body felt strange, somehow not the same. She continued her struggle until at last her head broke out into the cool air. As the rest of her body appeared, she realised why she felt different. She had grown wings! Delicate, milky wings that drooped at her sides.

She rested, tired from her pushing. After a while she began to feel stronger. She stretched and spread her wings, and suddenly she began to flutter. At last with one supreme effort she became airborne and flew into the sunbeams that streamed through her window. 'How beautiful I am!' she cried.

'Wake up, Lorraine! Wake up!' Her mother was picking up all the blankets which Lorraine had flung off her bed. 'Good heavens, child! You were tossing and turning like a ship in a storm. How are you feeling today, honey?'

'I dreamt I was a silkworm; that I was all bound up in my cocoon and was trying to wriggle out. When I did, I had changed into a silkmoth with wings! It was wonderful, Mum! I was flying!' whispered Lorraine huskily.

Lorraine had tonsilitis and had been in bed for a few days now. Her throat hurt terribly and her head was burning.

'When will I be better?' she asked desperately. 'My silkworms might be making their cocoons, and I'm missing it all. The old lady will think I don't care any more.' Lorraine began to cry.

'You're certainly not better yet, my girl. You just stay put in bed. I'm off to work now, but Aunty Violet will look after you.'

Lorraine sank back into her pillows as her mother straightened out her bed and tucked in the blankets. Then she hurried away and Lorraine dozed off. After awhile she woke to hear Aunty Violet moving round in the living room.

'Oh Aunty Vi!' she wailed. 'I do so want to see my pets before they fly away.'

'Then you just better take your medicine and hurry up and get better,' said her Aunt, coming in and giving her a kiss.

It seemed a very long time before Lorraine was better, but at last the day came when she was fit for school. The very next Saturday she went looking for Franklyn at the bus station.

'Can I go with you on the bus today?' asked Lorraine. 'I must go to the old lady and see how my silkworms are getting on.'

'Sure you can come!' said Franklyn warmly. 'It's nice to see you better at last. I thought I saw your friend the old lady just the other day. I would have stopped to tell her you were ill, but I was running late that day.'

Lorraine got on the bus and sat at the corner near the entrance. As the bus set off once more along the familiar route, she thought how strange that it all appeared so new again, just like the first day! She seemed to look with new eyes at the bustling shops of the High Street and the market; the little streets with their rows of houses and then the way the road and sky seemed to broaden together as they passed the playing fields and the bus began to climb the hill.

When Lorraine arrived at the old lady's

house, she found it looking even more over-grown and uncared for than before. She could barely see the big bay window through the mulberry tree, and a strange stillness made her pause at the gate, as nervous as she had been the first time.

At last she pushed open the garden gate and walked up the path, kicking aside the straggles of weeds that threatened to trip her up. She rang the bell as she had always done, and heard it echoing all the way through the house into the distance. She waited; the old lady did not appear at the window as usual to greet her before opening the door.

Lorraine was about to go when she noticed the door was slightly open, so after a moment's hesitation, she went in. To her surprise, the old lady was standing in the hall, so pale in the sunlight that she looked as if she would fade away.

'The silkworms!' burst out Lorraine. 'Are they all right? Have they gone?'

'The moths have flown, my dear,' murmured the old lady in a soft, silvery voice, 'all except one. It stayed longer in the cocoon, for it is not quite strong enough yet. We have both been waiting for you to come.'

Lorraine followed the old lady through the house to the conservatory. Once more she could smell the rich scent of geraniums and tomatoes, and there on the ledge was the cardboard box with the cocoons lying broken and empty.

'I've missed everything,' cried Lorraine. 'I couldn't come before because I was ill.' She picked up one of the cocoons and held it sadly in the palm of her hand, feeling its silkiness.

'No, my dear, you have not missed it all – look!' cried the old lady, pointing towards one corner. 'There is the silkmoth that waited for you!'

Lorraine turned her head eagerly. There, resting on a large mulberry leaf, was a newly-hatched silkmoth. It was still exhausted with the struggle and was panting as it warmed itself in the sunlight, waiting for the strength to fly away.

'Nibble, nibble, hungry lady,
Eat through the dark green leaves.
Though you munch your own green home,
Think what households you'll enrich,' whispered the old lady, as if to herself.

At that moment, the last silkmoth suddenly stretched itself. Its wings spread outwards, sparkling in the light. Then it fluttered past them and away.

'Now it is time for me to go too,' said the

old lady quietly. She raised her hand in fare-well.

'Goodbye!' said Lorraine. 'Even though the silkmoths have flown, I would like to see you again.'

The old lady did not reply but smiled a gentle smile as Lorraine turned and made her way back through the dark house and out into the garden, closing the front door softly be-hind her.

The following weekend Lorraine sat in her usual place on the bus, near to Franklyn, and waited patiently for the bus to climb the hill to the old lady's house. She was carrying a bag of mangoes for the old lady and was looking forward to sharing them with her.

As the big houses at the top of the hill came into view, Lorraine jumped up happily.

'See you later, Franklyn ... *Franklyn!* ...' Her voice turned to a shriek. 'The mulberry tree! It's gone!'

Her scream turned the heads of the other passengers who all looked out of the window.

Franklyn whistled with surprise. 'That's what I call a transformation.'

The mulberry tree had been cut right down so that not even a stump remained to show it had ever been there. Even the house itself looked different. It had been painted in shining colours, and now that the mulberry tree had gone the windows looked out boldly with cool, unfriendly eyes.

'They've done a good job with that old house,' exclaimed one of the passengers.

'Such a shame the way it was allowed to rot like that – spoiled the rest of the road,' said another.

'I never could understand how the old lady put up with that terrible tree in front of her windows, blocking out all the light. I'd have chopped it down years ago,' added a third.

'Has the old lady moved?' asked Franklyn.

'Dear me, no!' said one of the passengers. 'She died three weeks ago. Her daughter's returned from abroad to take on the house.'

'Died three weeks ago!' Franklyn and Lorraine looked at each other in astonishment.

'That's impossible! You saw her last week, didn't you, Lorraine?' asked Franklyn.

'She told me she had been waiting for me. She and the last silkmoth – they had been waiting for me to come,' whispered Lorraine. She leaned back in her seat in bewilderment, as the bus went slowly past the house.

'I think that old lady thought a lot of you,' said Franklyn comfortingly. 'So much so, that she did wait for you, so that you would not miss the miracle she had told you about. Do you still want to get off, Lorraine?'

'No, I won't get off,' said Lorraine, 'I'll just stay with you until we go back home.'

Monday morning came, the same as all Monday mornings, rushing about, trying to shake off the weekend, getting ready for school and work. They were all late as usual. Dad had just rushed out, dragging on his jacket, and Mum was clearing the table round Lorraine, flinging the dishes into the sink, when suddenly they heard a key turn in the lock and Dad's voice shouting excitedly.

'What's Dad doing back?' asked Lorraine, quickly gobbling down the last mouthful.

'I don't know,' cried Mum with alarm. 'Is anything wrong?' she called.

But Lorraine saw that nothing could be wrong. Her father was standing there with the biggest grin on his face that she had ever seen. He was waving a letter in the air.

'It's come at last!' he shouted joyfully. 'The letter from the Housing Department. We have a house! We can move in two weeks!' Lorraine, her mother and father all hugged each other with delight.

'We're coming down from the clouds at last!' laughed Mum. 'We're going to have our own front door, and our own little garden.'

'Jeepers! Does that mean I'll have to mow the grass?' groaned Dad.

'We'll have neighbours to chat to over the wall, and Lorraine can pop out to play easy as pie, without going down eleven floors and me being worried to death all the time,' said Mum.

'And one thing we might consider, Lorraine, my honey!' said Dad mysteriously.

'What Dad? What?' gasped Lorraine.

'As you are allowed to keep pets in council houses, I think we'll let you have a rabbit or a kitten.'

Lorraine looked as if she was going to burst! She jumped up and down. 'A rabbit or a kitten,' she chanted, 'or why not a monkey? I always wanted a monkey.'

'Why not an alligator or a thirty-foot python?' added Dad. 'Anything is possible now we have a house!'

Then Lorraine stopped laughing and jumping about, and said more seriously, 'I think though, just to begin with, I'd really like some more silkworms, and, Dad, do you think the council would mind us planting a mulberry tree in our garden?'

2 Over-The-Log

The disco music from Joyce's record-player thumped through the flat and Charlie was rushing from room to room making 'Vroom! Vroom!' noises. At last their mother clasped her head and screamed, 'Out! Out! the lot of you! My head is bursting. Joyce, turn off that record-player before I throw it out of the window! Take Charlie to the swings!'

'Oh do I have to?' wailed Joyce sulkily. She was all prepared for an argument until she saw her mother's face. 'Oh, OK. Come on, Charlie.'

Charlie was pleased. He loved going out, especially to go along to the swings. He looked around for something to take with him, but Joyce yanked him out by his collar. 'Come on, pest!' she hissed. How she hated being landed with her brother.

They crossed the High Street and set off along Windsor Road. On each side were tall, crumbling houses with high steps that went up to large, peeling front doors, and low steps that went down to basements full of dustbins and prowling cats. Windsor Road did not lead to the park where the swings were.

'Hey! Joyce!' protested Charlie. 'I thought we were going to the swings!' Joyce didn't even bother to reply.

'Joyce!' repeated Charlie with a wail. Then he realised. They were going 'Over-The-Log!' That was different. Charlie ran on ahead. Joyce must have come down Windsor Road to get out of sight of their home, just in case Mum saw them going in the opposite direction to the swings.

'Over-The-Log' was the name the neighbourhood children gave to some waste ground round the corner from Windsor Road. A house had stood there once, but it had been bombed to pieces in the war, and a great horse-chestnut tree from the garden lay like a fallen giant across the muddy holes and craters.

The grownups told the children not to play there because they said it was dangerous. There was so much rubble and broken glass, and people dumped things there like old prams and fridges. But the kids took no notice. It was the best place to play.

There was still one large wall standing which went up at least two floors of the house. You could see where each room had been by the different scraps of wall-paper clinging to the wall; arches showed where there were fire-places, and a big zig-zag pattern across the brick marked the position of the staircase. Tall weeds straggled up the wall and filled in the craters, creating a wonderful jungle for hiding in, or a battle-scarred landscape for playing war games.

When they arrived at 'Over-The-Log', Joyce left Charlie and ran over to a gang of boys who were sitting on the old log, smoking and chatting. Pete was among them, and Joyce fancied Pete.

Charlie wandered about by himself. None of his friends was here. Never mind, he'd have another go on that swing he'd discovered at the far end. Funny how it didn't seem to be there all the time, and he'd never seen anyone else on it. But it was always there when he was alone. It was a nice one too, not like those at the park with cracked plastic seats and rusted chains. This had shiny, black chains that hung from a very high place – he wasn't sure from where – and the seat was wooden and painted white.

He sat on it and immediately felt happy. He pushed off gently. Some swings were hard to get going, but this one seemed to work all by itself. With hardly any effort, Charlie was going higher and higher, and he began chanting to himself, 'Is it a plane? Is it a bird? No, it's Super Charlie!'

Now he was so high he could see right across the waste ground. There was Joyce sitting on the log with Pete. He could see Pete's motorbike propped nearby. 'Ooh good!' thought Charlie. 'Perhaps he'll give me a ride later.'

He swung higher still, and now he was up among the shimmering leaves of a huge chestnut tree. The sun was shining strongly, making everything glint and sparkle. It made Charlie's eyes water to look into it, so he looked down again, and got the shock of his life!

Everything had changed. Instead of the waste ground of 'Over-The-Log' he was swinging over a beautiful, smooth, green lawn; instead of the huge, fallen log there was a tall, spreading chestnut tree with the blue sky peeping through the leaves and he himself swinging from one of the branches! Where had Joyce and Pete got to? And all the other kids?

He looked all round but they were nowhere

to be seen. Instead, there was an enormous, old-fashioned house with tall, reflecting windows and little, iron-wrought balconies. It had sloping roofs and turrets, which reminded him of a fairy tale castle, and clusters of tall chimneys from which wisps of smoke coiled into the air.

Suddenly, the glass doors of the conservatory flew open and some children came tumbling out, laughing and chattering. Charlie had never seen these kids before. They weren't from round here, he was sure of that. Why, they didn't even look like anyone he had ever seen before.

Perhaps they were foreign? Their clothes were so strange. Or perhaps they were at a Fancy Dress party? The girls wore long, silky dresses which stuck out all round over tons of frilly petticoat, and the boy wore trousers down to the knee, then stockings and buckled shoes. He also wore a waistcoat over a full shirt with a bow tied at the collar.

Charlie stopped swinging his legs and gaped in amazement as the children chased across the grass to a round, stone pond with a statue of a cherub in the middle with water bubbling from its mouth.

But, as the swing slowed down, the scene below him began to fade. Charlie couldn't

41

understand what was happening at first, but he discovered that by swinging his legs again and taking the swing upwards, the lawn and the children reappeared.

Before he had time to consider the strangeness of this, a voice rang out. 'Look! There's a strange boy on our swing – *and* he's black!'

Charlie stopped swinging, he was so shocked. As the scene below him faded, he could just hear a distant voice replying, 'Don't be silly, there's no one there.' The sounds of their voices merged and lost themselves with the roar of a motorbike.

Charlie slowed down and down until the swing stopped. He was back 'Over-The-Log' and one of Pete's friends had arrived on his motorbike.

Joyce was still sitting there on the log, and Charlie noted with satisfaction that she and Pete were holding hands. That meant they wouldn't be going home just yet!

Charlie sat on the swing, motionless. He must have been daydreaming he decided. He looked up into the sky. There were no broad, leafy branches of a chestnut tree, only the faint, silver speck of a jet airliner trailing across a clear sky.

Charlie pushed off again, leaning forwards and backwards, forwards and backwards, urging the swing onwards and upwards. Higher and higher he went till, suddenly, there he was again, up among the rustling, green leaves of the chestnut tree.

Suddenly a shrill voice rang out as before. 'Look! There's that black boy on our swing again!'

All the children stopped running and stared. Charlie looked at them and they looked at him.

'Blimy! They're real!' he muttered. He did not stop swinging as he felt safer staying well up, out of reach.

The children advanced towards him rather menacingly and Charlie felt a bit scared.

'What, pray, are you doing on our swing?' demanded the boy in an oddly commanding voice, though he only looked about eleven years old.

'I didn't know it was your swing. I came 'Over-The-Log' with my sister, Joyce. She's down there somewhere with Pete,' replied Charlie shakily. He was still a bit scared, and he wasn't sure that they would all go away if he slowed down.

'I think you are lying,' said the boy. 'There is no one else here. You are an intruder. I will summon the servants to throw you out.'

'Do what you like!' yelled Charlie, feeling braver because he was annoyed. 'None of you is here anyway when I'm not swinging. If I stopped, you would all disappear.'

'What does he mean?' exploded one of the girls.

'Even your house and garden will disappear,' Charlie went on. 'All this is just a pile of rubble – a bomb-site!'

'The boy must be mad,' said the girl with a prim, grown-up voice. 'Cecil, call nurse!'

'Wait, Charlotte,' said the boy. 'He says he can make us disappear. Go on then! Do it!' he taunted.

Immediately, Charlie began to slow down. He let his legs dangle and, as he gradually began to drop lower, he prayed fervently that they would all go away.

Then he heard their voices squealing in astonishment, 'He's disappearing! Quick! Call him back!'

As their excited voices began to die away, Charlie could just hear Cecil calling, 'Come back! Come back! Please come back. We won't call out the servants.'

So Charlie swung his legs again and, as he

rose higher, the chestnut tree reappeared and the children's incredulous faces sharpened into focus.

'It's you who disappears!' Cecil suddenly burst out triumphantly, 'not us!'

'No, I don't, you do,' retorted Charlie huffily.

'Does that make sense?' asked the youngest, whose name was Amelia.

'It shouldn't, I don't think, but on this occasion it seems to,' replied Charlotte.

Cecil looked excited. He began hopping up and down and running under the swing, trying to touch it as it swooped back and forth.

'It would be grand if you could come down somehow without us all disappearing from each other,' he cried. 'I'd like to talk to you. You must be some sort of genie.'

Amelia giggled with delight at this idea. 'Did you come out of a lamp, oh, did you?'

'Shut up, silly,' Charlotte said, reprimanding her little sister. 'You'll hurt his feelings.'

Cecil stopped hopping about and leaned against the trunk, looking up at Charlie who was now beginning to feel a little foolish.

'I say, boy – er – whatsyourname?'

'Charlie,' said Charlie.

'Er ... Charlie, I know you are rather high up when you are visible to us, but what if you

slowed down as far as possible, just to the point before you begin to vanish, and if at that moment you jumped off the swing, would it work, do you think?' he asked.

The girls looked shocked. 'Cecil! What a suggestion!' cried Charlotte.

'He might get smashed to pieces,' breathed Amelia. 'Then what would nursie say?'

Cecil took no notice of his sisters but went on staring boldly up at Charlie. 'Are you scared?' he asked with a sneer.

'I'll come down and fight you,' choked Charlie, the anger rushing up inside him.

'Watch out!' And, without giving it any further consideration, Charlie launched himself through the air.

As he let go of the chains, the air seemed to swirl round him. He felt like a bug being sucked down a plughole, or a spaceship caught up in a black hole. He seemed to be flying through space for ever but then, with an immense thud that knocked all the wind out of him, he landed on the grass at the feet of the three children.

There was a dreadful silence for a second or

two as the children gazed in horror at the boy lying prone at their feet.

'We've killed him!' whispered Charlotte, her voice trembling with tears.

Amelia began to cry. 'What shall we do? What will nursie say, oh, what will nursie say?'

'Shut up, both of you,' rasped Cecil hoarsely, although he was terrified to the pit of his stomach. 'It's not my fault. I didn't make him do it!'

'You shouldn't have dared him,' cried Charlotte. 'Oh dear! What shall we do?'

Suddenly, Charlie gave a huge, quivering sigh and opened his eyes.

'Where's Joyce?' Charlie muttered, trying to see through the mists drifting before his eyes.

'He's not dead after all! Oh thank God!' exclaimed Charlotte with relief.

Charlie shut his eyes then opened them again. 'Did it work then?' he whispered, 'Am I with you lot?'

'You most certainly are,' replied Cecil in a voice which suggested that he didn't know if that were a good thing or a bad thing.

Charlie sat up. The children fell back, feeling suddenly shy and half afraid.

'Are you really a ghost?' asked Amelia tremulously.

'Don't be daft,' said Charlie struggling to his feet. 'Do I look like one?'

'I could try walking through him,' suggested Cecil.

'Don't be silly,' snapped Charlotte. Then she turned to Charlie.

'Perhaps you could start by telling us where you come from and who you are?'

'I come from down the road there – you know – Laburnum Grove. We live in those flats at the bottom, Jubilee House,' Charlie said.

Then, when he saw the blank, incomprehending faces of the children, he said, 'You must know! It's just two minutes from here. Cross over the zebra crossing, turn left by the fish and chip shop and go down Windsor Road ...'

'Are you mad?' interrupted Charlotte.

'Or a liar!' exclaimed Cecil. 'There's no such place as Laburnum Grove, and what flats are you talking about? Do you mean the marshes?'

'Have you just come from Africa?' continued Charlotte, trying to puzzle him out, with all his talk of zebras and fish shops. 'You're not a runaway slave are you? Shall we call the servants? You'll be flogged you know.'

That did it. Charlie turned furiously on his heel and marched towards the swing.

'I'm going home. You're just talking rubbish. Try calling your servants. Just you see, I'll call Pete and his mates. Pete's a karate expert; he could deal with ten men *and* he's got a motorbike.'

Charlie reached the swing and began to push off. His heart was beating wildly with fear and anger. What had he got himself into?

'What's a motorbike?' asked Amelia in a small voice.

Charlotte ran forward. 'Oh Charlie, don't go,' she begged. Suddenly she had stopped being grown-up or prissy. 'We don't understand the words you are using. We'll try not to be rude. Of course we won't call the servants, so please don't go yet.'

Charlie stayed on the swing because he felt safer there, but he said, 'OK. OK.' He sat in silence for a moment looking at Charlotte, then beyond her to Cecil and Amelia, and all around him. The grand house seemed more like a palace, with its huge, wide, velvet-like lawns.

'Looks like Buckingham Palace,' muttered

Charlie uneasily. 'Are you royalty? You look it in those clothes. And what's that about servants?'

'No, you aren't at Buckingham Palace; we aren't royalty, not remotely. Father is a merchant. What's so odd about servants? You must be one,' said Charlotte.

She was trying to be nice, but at that remark Charlie looked furious again and shuffled on the swing as if about to take off.

'Oh dear!' she sighed, 'something is very strange. I understand the words you use – well, most of them – but I don't understand your meaning.'

'I don't understand you at all,' grumbled Charlie. 'All I know is, I'm Charlie Miles. I've come down here with my sister, Joyce. We live at 52 Jubilee House, Laburnum Grove, and we call this place 'Over-The-Log' because usually you lot aren't here. This place is just a dump, a bomb site. See?

There's no house, no garden and no tree; well, the tree's been cut down and there's only the log. And I don't know anyone with servants. Only royalty have them, or very, very rich people. Anyway, I'm not one. Dad works at a paint factory and Mum serves in a café, but she's not a servant, and Joyce and me, we're at school.'

'I see,' said Charlotte blankly but feeling like the blind man who couldn't see at all. 'But we are always here. So is our house and garden and everything. We've never come and gone as you seem to. Our name is Orpington, Charlotte, Cecil and Amelia,' she said, indicating herself, her brother and sister.

'Of course we have servants; everyone does except the very, very poor, though we don't have many. We only keep two gardeners, a groom, a cook, a house-keeper, a butler, a manservant, three housemaids, a lady's maid and a young girl who helps with the fires and things like that. Oh, and of course there's our governess, Miss April.

We don't go to school, though Cecil is going next Autumn. Mrs. Redburn comes in to teach us music and painting, Professor Blenke teaches us Physics and Chemistry, and the Reverend Armitage gives us religious instruction and teaches us Latin and Greek.'

'Crumbs!' was all Charlie could say.

'I say!' interrupted Cecil, who had been following the conversation with an intense frown on his face. 'I have a serious and fascinating proposition to put to you. Speaking of Professor Blenke reminded me,' he went on. 'I heard him and father talking in the library the other night. They were discussing Time, the stars and the universe, but especially Time. I didn't understand half the words they were using, and Professor Blenke kept quoting mathematical formulas and stuff, but he was mainly discussing the possibility of finding ways to travel into the past or the future.

Father wondered if it was very wrong, and hoped the vicar didn't get to hear about such ideas, but Professor Blenke laughed and said it was nothing to do with religion, it was just Science. He talked about people who say they have seen ghosts, and he said, "what if they were not ghosts at all, but people who had slipped out of one time into another!'"

'I say!' breathed Charlotte. 'What a proposition indeed!'

'Cor!' gasped Charlie, feeling frightfully important. 'Does that make me a Time Traveller?'

'I think that's boring,' pouted Amelia. 'I want Charlie to be a ghost, that's much more exciting. Come on, Charlie! Chase us!' she pleaded, then ran giggling with pleasure down towards the fountain, with the others close behind.

*　　*　　*

Soon all the children were weaving in and out of the shrubbery, laughing and shrieking, while Charlie chased them, waving his arms about and hooting like a ghost.

Panting and hot, he at last raced over to the fountain and, tearing off his shoes and socks, jumped into the pond!

The children stopped in amazement. 'Charlie! You are a bad boy indeed!' exclaimed Charlotte severely.

'Get out, Charlie,' begged Amelia. 'If nursie sees you it will mean a whipping.'

Charlie kicked the water up, sending the spray in a wide arc. 'Oh, come on, scaredy cats! It's great! Come on in and cool down. Come on, Cecil!' he chortled.

'It is forbidden!' replied Cecil, who was really longing to go in.

'Dare you, dare you!' taunted Charlie, now getting his own back on Cecil.

Cecil glanced anxiously towards the house, then quickly removed his shoes and stockings. 'Now we're equal!' he shouted, triumphantly leaping into the fountain.

Soon there was pandemonium as Charlie and Cecil chased each other round and round the cherub, kicking up water and splashing each other till they were soaked to the skin. The girls, too, got drawn into the game, running in close, then dashing away to avoid a well-aimed shower of water. No one noticed a figure appear in the doorway of the conservatory; a broad, bosomy lady who came bearing down the garden towards them like a galleon in full sail.

Amelia saw her first and promptly burst into tears. Charlotte gasped in horror, 'Cecil! Get out, quickly – it's nurse!'

'Master Cecil!' The voice boomed out with such power and authority that even Charlie was halted in his tracks and gaped at the large, full-skirted, bonneted lady who towered over them like an ogress. 'OUT!' she bellowed. 'OUT, I say!'

Cecil climbed out swiftly and silently and gathered together his shoes and stockings. Charlie hung back, hoping to sidle round the back of the cherub and then make a dash for it, but nurse was too quick for him. As if reading his mind, she stretched out a long arm and hauled him out, her fingers pressing into his neck with the grip of a vice.

'And what heathen ragamuffin is this?' she shrieked.

Charlie closed his eyes as her fingers dug into his neck. 'I wish I really was a ghost,' he thought, 'Then I could just disappear.' But no matter how hard he tried, he could not will her away.

'Begone to the nursery!' she ordered the three children. 'Bradley will deal with this intruder.' She squeezed Charlie's neck on the word "this" so that he couldn't help giving a cry of pain.

Cecil, Charlotte and Amelia walked meekly towards the house, to await the severe punishment they would undoubtedly receive. Nurse dragged Charlie towards a side door which led to the kitchens. He was yelling and shouting and making a terrible rumpus.

'I'll make you all disappear! I'll get Pete and his mates to sort you out – or my dad! Don't you dare lay a hand on me. I don't belong in your time ... OW ... OW ... you can't treat me like this ... OW!' His threats turned to shrieks as he was struck across the head.

A man appeared, and the nurse thrust Charlie towards him.

'Parkin! we have an intruder. This boy is either a servant from Mr. Carrington's household or he's a runaway slave from one of the ships down at the port. Either way, he's an intruder and should be whipped. Get Bradley to see to it!'

As Charlie was handed over to the man-servant, Parkin, he threw one last glance in the direction of the children. They were just going into the conservatory, but before he was lost from sight Cecil paused, looked at Charlie and gave a slight, sympathetic shrug, then hurried away as nurse swept up behind him.

Charlie felt as if he were in the middle of a nightmare. If this is what happened when you went into another Time, then he'd never do it again, that's for sure. If only he hadn't gone on that stupid swing. What if he never got back?

Luckily Mr. Bradley, the butler, was out, so Charlie was spared a whipping but he was shoved roughly into the broom closet with the buckets and mops and the door was locked.

When Mr. Bradley did return, Charlie was dragged out for questioning. Enquiries had already been made in the surrounding neighbourhood, but no one had heard of any boy fitting Charlie's description, not even Mr. Carrington who was against the slave trade and thought it should be abolished.

'Come on, you varmint!' growled Mr. Bradley. 'Where did you run away from? Whose servant are you?'

But the more Charlie protested that he was neither servant nor slave, the more they called him a liar.

'Is it possible that he has escaped from one of the slave ships down at the port?' nurse said later.

'If I don't hear any more on his ownership by tomorrow, I'll take him down to the port and hand him over to one of the captains,' replied Mr. Bradley. 'They can ship him to America and no doubt get a penny or two for him – he's quite a strapping lad.'

Flung back into the broom cupboard once more, Charlie began to realise the danger he was in. He could hear the chatter of the kitchen girls through the door.

'I reckon the boy's mad,' one girl said. 'Keeps talking about not being of this Time. Well I mean, that's mad talk or blasphemy. It's the madhouse for him, I say.'

'Never!' said another. 'He's valuable. You mark my words, Bradley will hand him over to a slaver and get a crown or two for him.'

'Poor kid! Either way, he's not got much of a life to look forward to.'

The hours passed by, and at last the kitchen noises died away as night came and the last of the servants went to bed.

Huddled inside the cupboard, all Charlie could hear was the low, steady ticking of the kitchen clock, and the snuffly snores of an old dog whose bed was in front of the kitchen hearth.

'I must get back to the swing,' he muttered to himself, clutching his stomach as if to squeeze back the panic inside him. But how? The cupboard door was locked fast and there was no window. He would have suffocated but for the gap under the door. Tears of despair filled his eyes.

Suddenly, he heard a slight noise. The dog heard it too, and stirred. Then he heard a voice soothing the dog in a whisper. 'Shhh! Bessie, good girl.' There was a soft clicking of a key turning in a well oiled lock, and to Charlie's joy the door swung open.

A shaft of moonlight lit up the doorway, and there stood Cecil in his nightshirt.

'Come on quickly. You must flee from here, or it will be the worse for you.' He took his arm and pulled Charlie out of the cupboard. 'Follow me!'

'Blimy, Cecil!' croaked Charlie. 'I thought I'd had it!'

Cecil had a small, flickering candle in a candle holder. He led Charlie out of the kitchen and down a long, dark, stone corridor, shielding the flame all the time in case it should blow out.

At last they reached an arched door.

'Hold this,' ordered Cecil, handing Charlie the candle.

Charlie took it while Cecil fumbled in his night-shirt pocket and drew out a huge, iron key. He thrust the key into the lock, but this one was stiff and an age seemed to pass while he rattled and pushed it.

Far away, down the passage behind them, Bessie began barking again.

'Hurry! Hurry!' gasped Charlie. 'Oh, please be quick!'

Cecil desperately forced the key in once more and gave a massive twist! At last the key turned, creaking loudly in the lock.

'It's done!' exclaimed Cecil. He leaned against the old, wooden door and pushed with his whole weight. Slowly it swung open.

As the boys rushed out into the night, Bessie's barks became more and more frantic. Voices were heard shouting inside the house, and the glow of candles could be seen at some of the windows.

Cecil and Charlie were standing in the vegetable garden to the side of the house.

'Follow me!' cried Cecil, and began to run down a path between the cabbages. At the far end of the vegetable garden, they reached a high, red brick wall. Cecil pushed open yet another door, and at last they were back in the garden.

'Do you know where you are?' asked Cecil urgently.

'Yes! Yes! The swing's down there, isn't it? Yes – there – I can see the fountain.'

'Run then, run!' whispered Cecil, hoarsely, 'and Charlie ...' his voice suddenly changed, 'Charlie ... God go with thee!'

Then Cecil turned and disappeared back through the door into the vegetable garden and was gone.

Charlie ran as he'd never run before. He ran straight across the lawn while behind him more lights appeared, shouting voices mingled with the barking of dogs. Ahead of him loomed the giant body of the chestnut tree and there also was the swing!

Charlie cried out with relief. He raced across the grass towards it, only dimly aware that he could feel the dew between his toes because he had left his shoes and socks by the fountain.

As he reached the swing, the conservatory door was flung open and a large dog came bounding down towards him. But it was too late! Charlie had jumped on the swing and pushed off. Its easy motion did not let him down. Within seconds he was up and away, swinging high among the chestnut leaves which gleamed luminously in the moonlight.

At the highest point of the swing, the moon became the sun. The leaves faded, and Charlie looked down once more on the battered landscape of 'Over-The-Log'. The swing slowed down to a halt and Charlie slid off and moved away from it quickly, afraid that some power might drag him back and snatch him away.

He turned and ran, leaping the mounds of scattered brick to where Joyce and Pete were still sitting hand in hand.

'Hi! Joyce!' called Charlie, bracing himself for a ticking off for disappearing for hours like that.

'Hello, Charlie!' replied Joyce indifferently. 'I suppose we ought to be going.' Then she saw his strained face and wild eyes; and she saw his soaked clothes and bare feet.

'Charlie!' she screamed. 'What the blazes have you been up to? Where are your shoes?'

'I've lost them,' grunted Charlie, trying frantically to think up some excuse.

'I took them off because my feet were feeling

sticky and this dog came along, and he run off with them.'

Joyce fumed and fretted, reluctantly leaving Pete's side to go and search for Charlie's shoes, but it was no use.

'What are you going to do?' she wailed. 'You can't go home like that; Mum will be mad! She'll blame me, I know she will, she always does! Why are you such a pest, Charlie Miles?' she bleated, giving Charlie a cuff round the ear.

'Lay off, Joyce!' said Pete, giving Charlie a wink. 'I'll take the kid home on my motor-bike.'

'Oh Pete, thanks!' cried Charlie joyfully. For that treat it was worth even the risk of being sold off as a slave!

Their mother was out when Charlie got home. He sighed with relief and quickly put on a pair of dry trousers and found his old daps to wear. With luck she wouldn't notice the loss of his shoes for a while.

Later, over tea, Charlie said to his dad, 'I'm glad we're alive today and not in the past, otherwise we might have been slaves!'

'Charlie Miles!' exclaimed his mum. 'Who's been getting at you? Don't you take any cheek from people. You are equal to any man. You were born here . . .'

'Mum!' pleaded Charlie, 'No one's got at me. I just said I'm glad I live now – that's all!'

'Quite right,' agreed Dad. 'Things may be tough in the present day, but there's not much in the past I'd care to exchange it for.'

When Charlie had finished his tea, he felt restless. He wandered over to the window and saw that the sunny afternoon had given way to a steady drizzle. In the darkening evening people were hurrying home, their heads bent against the fine rain which Charlie could see slanting against the orange glow of the sodium street lighting.

Was it raining 'Over-The-Log'? Over and beyond in the other Time? Suddenly Charlie gasped. There was a familiar-looking boy standing in the orange spotlight of the lamp-post, with the rain falling around him like a veil. His pale face was turned upwards towards Charlie's window, yet he gave no sign of having seen him.

'Cecil!' Charlie gasped. Surely it was he! He was wearing the same sort of fancy dress clothes with the buckled shoes. People hurried by but no one threw him a glance or seemed to notice the strangeness of his clothes.

Charlie dashed out of the flat and down the stairs two at a time. He ran out into the street calling, 'Cecil! Cecil!' He stopped, confused

and disappointed. There was no one under the lamp-post. The pool of light made by the orange lamp was empty.

Charlie looked up and down the street, but there was no boy to be seen. He walked slowly towards the lamp-post. Wait a moment! There was something on the pavement. Charlie gasped with amazement.

'My shoes! Cecil brought back my shoes!'

There was the sound of a window being thrown open, and Charlie's mother leaned out.

'Charlie! What on earth are you doing out in the rain? Get back in here this minute before you catch your death of cold!'

It was a week before Charlie went back 'Over-The-Log', but in the meantime he had heard the news. 'Over-The-Log' didn't exist anymore. That week the bulldozers had moved in. A fence went up all round the site; giant cranes towered like dinosaurs, and earth-movers gobbled up the rubble in their teeth like hungry monsters. They were building an office block, and the swing had gone.

3 Double Dare

Terry couldn't remember a time when he wasn't at Julian Road Children's Home. He used to try very hard, because he felt that if he could remember his life before the children's home he might remember his mother.

'You do have to have a mother to be born, don't you?' he once asked Aunty Eileen, who ran the home.

'You weren't left by the storks, dear, if that's what you mean,' she laughed, but bustled away before he could ask any more questions.

'You've got to have a father, too,' said his friend, Paul, who seemed to know a lot more about these things than Terry. This may have been because Paul had a mum. She visited him sometimes, but only sometimes, and it didn't seem to make Paul any happier. Usually it made him sadder. His mum had let him down too often. She was always saying, 'See you on Saturday,' then not turn up.

Terry didn't suppose she knew or cared that Paul would have been up since five in the morning, fully dressed with his coat on, waiting for her by the door.

But Terry supposed there must be some advantage in having a mother, or at least being able to say you had one. But so far as he knew he had nobody, neither mother nor father nor brothers nor sisters, nor anyone whom he could really call family.

What he did have was an abundance of aunts and uncles, none of whom really were! It was just what you called the grownups who looked after you or who took a special interest in you.

Like Aunt May, for instance. She was Terry's own special aunt. She took him out about once a fortnight, and when she said she was coming, she came.

She would arrive in her little, white Mini and drive him to her house for tea. She lived in a neat, little terraced house, with a neat, little garden in front, full of rose bushes set into concrete, and a neat, little garden at the back which she called her pocket handkerchief because it was small for a back garden.

Sometimes she took Terry to the zoo, or up the Thames on a steamer. And if the circus was coming round she would take him *and* one of his friends. So she was quite nice as aunts go and better than some of the mothers he had heard of.

When he thought about it, Terry would ask her questions. Once, he had asked, 'Why am I half and half?'

And Aunt May had laughed and said jokingly, 'because you are half good and half bad!' Then she added more seriously, 'because you aren't all English. Your father came from India.'

'What was my mother's name?' asked Terry.

Aunt May shrugged her shoulders sadly. 'I'm sorry, Terry, I don't know.'

Terry didn't mind. He had given his mother a name anyway, Angela, and he might have been disappointed to find out it was something else.

In time, Terry discovered that his mother was called Sandra, not Angela; that his father came from India to study, had met and married his mother, and then a year later he had been killed in a motorcycle accident.

Sandra was completely unable to bring up a baby on her own and her family wouldn't

69

help her, so she handed Terry over to a Children's Home saying she would be back, but she never came back nor made any kind of contact.

So Terry grew up with only a vague idea about mothers and fathers and families. They just seemed to be things that other people had.

It was after school one day, when Terry was in the park, racing round on his bike with his friends, that he suddenly noticed a dark, elderly man, sitting cross-legged under one of the tall, plane trees.

'Funny, he wasn't there just now,' thought Terry to himself, looking with interest at this somewhat odd character, who had a white turban wrapped round his head. He wore a tweedy-looking overcoat, which seemed too big for him, white, wrinkly pyjamas and he had a long, flowing, grey beard in which silver strands danced and sparkled.

His eyes were closed, and the palms of his hands, which rested loosely over his knees, were turned upwards, with the thumb and first finger lightly touching. Laid in front of him was a black, rolled-up umbrella.

'He must be praying, or something,' thought Terry, remembering an advertisement he had seen in the London underground of a holy man sitting like that.

He turned to see where his friends were, but they were far across the other side of the playing fields, and when he turned round again, the old man had gone – just vanished into thin air!

For a moment Terry stood there, feeling a little foolish and puzzled, then he jumped on his bike and rode off to chase his friends, 'yahooing' like a cowboy.

He didn't think about the old man again until just before he fell asleep that night. 'I wonder where that old bloke disappeared to?' he muttered to himself, as he drifted off.

The next morning, Terry nudged and jostled his friends as usual at the bus stop. Every day they caught the 209 to school, and there was always a stampede to be the first up the steps to the top deck.

Terry, being small and wiry, often wriggled his way between his mates and got there first, determined to get either a seat at the very front or one at the very back. This morning he was first again.

He charged up the metalled steps, saw that the front seats were already full of clamouring school children, and swung round to claim a seat at the back.

But then he froze in astonishment, for there, sitting in the back, was the same old man he had seen sitting in the park the day before. He was in the same position, sitting cross-legged; his feet bare, his hands resting on his knees with the palms turned upwards and the thumbs and first fingers touching. Finally, almost as if it hung suspended, the black, rolled umbrella lay horizontally before him.

Despite the clamour, his eyes were closed, and nothing about the old man had changed except that now he was on top of the 209 bus instead of under a plane tree in the park.

'Get on, Terry!' someone yelled, as they all piled up behind him on the steps.

A rough shove sent him stumbling to his knees, and his mates clambered over him and bagged all the places.

The bus lurched forwards and Terry struggled to his feet. All the seats had gone – and so had the old man! He looked up and down the bus, and even between the seats.

'What are you doing, Loony?' yelled one of his friends, good naturedly.

'Looking for someone,' replied Terry, perplexed.

'Smuggling in illegal immigrants, are you!' joked another, and they all laughed.

'No standing on top!' bellowed the bus conductor above the din, and he pointed a finger at Terry to get below. Disconsolately, Terry clattered downstairs and hung on to the pole till they reached the school. As they all piled off the bus outside the school gates, the conductor heaved a sigh of relief, pressed the buzzer and gave his first smile of the morning.

In the classroom, Terry was greeted by his best friend, Alan.

'Hey, Tel!' yelled Alan, clambering over the desks towards him. 'Have you seen? That new Space Wars film has opened in Leicester Square! We've got to see it!'

'Yeh!' growled Terry, 'and what do we do for money? I'll have to wait till it comes out to our local cinema.'

'I'm not waiting that long!' declared Alan. 'In fact I think I'll go today. I want to be first in the school to see it, and you too!'

'You what? Me!' exclaimed Terry, aghast. 'How?' But before they could continue their conversation, the teacher came in and told everyone to get back to their seats.

During break, Alan came over to Terry with an expression on his face, which to Terry spelt mischief.

'Hey, Tel!' he called out cheerfully. 'Play "Truth, Dare, Double Dare, Love, Kiss or Promise!"'

'Come off it, Al! What are you up to?' asked Terry suspiciously.

'I just feel like playing it, that's all!' retorted Alan with a smile. 'What's wrong? Afraid I'll ask you to kiss Amanda Roberts?'

'Aw! Shut up!' groaned Terry, blushing.

'Come on, then!' nagged Alan. And he went on nagging till Terry relented, saying, 'I'll call first, then.' Alan beamed in agreement. 'Truth, Dare, Double Dare, Love, Kiss or Promise?'

'Truth!' shouted Alan.

'Is it true that you are going to the pictures?' asked Terry.

'Yes! It's true!' cried Alan triumphantly.

'But how?' asked Terry, enviously.

'No questions, just get on with the game. It's my turn now,' pressed Alan. 'Come on, Truth, Dare, Double Dare, Love, Kiss or Promise!'

'Double Dare!' muttered Terry, without thinking, and immediately regretted it. He could see by the look on Alan's face that he had picked exactly what Alan knew he would pick.

'Double Dare,' Alan said slowly, as if relishing the words. 'Right! The first dare is that I dare you to skive off school with me to go and see the new film in town!'

74

Terry sucked his breath in, astounded. 'Al
... you ...!' he exploded. 'Anyhow, I haven't
got the money.'

'Uh! Uh! I haven't finished yet,' gloated
Alan. 'Dare two – you get on the underground
without paying!'

Terry looked appalled. 'Oh no! You know
I did that once before and got caught!'

'You must have been an idiot. Only idiots
get caught. Besides, I know someone who does
it all the time! He never pays!' Alan informed
him tartly.

'You would!' choked Terry. 'And what
about getting into the film? It's only Double
Dare, remember? Not triple! I'm not sneaking
into the cinema. Am I supposed to stand
around outside for three hours while you're
inside enjoying yourself?'

'Come off it, Terry. We're pals aren't we? I
got five quid for my birthday. I could have
taken myself off to the flicks and done it all in
style, but it's no fun alone, so this is the best
answer. We do the underground and have
plenty for the movie. Anyway, there's no
arguments. I dared you. You've got to,' Alan
ended with an implacable tone in his voice,
'otherwise you'll get called "yellow, yellow!"
After all! I'm doing the Double Dare too, and
that's real friendship, I reckon.'

At that moment, a football came whizzing their way, and Alan lunged to intercept it.

As he got swept away into a game, Terry walked over to the school railings and pressed his head furiously against them. It was all right for Alan. He seemed to get away with everything. Last time they played that game, Terry had been dared to run across the track just when the train was on the bend.

He was seen by a passer-by and the police were called. He got into terrible trouble. The Social Services were called in, and so was the school. Terry was told that if he did such a silly thing again they might consider sending him to a special boarding school. But nothing happened to Alan.

On the pavement opposite, he noticed a young mother pushing a pram along with her shopping. 'She could be my mum,' he thought. He often played games like that.

He had even once followed a lady who was the sort of person he imagined his mother might look like. He had offered to carry her shopping basket, and then asked her if her name was Angela!

'Don't be cheeky!' she had retorted angrily, and flounced off. Anyway, now he knew he should have said Sandra.

He watched the woman until she had

pushed her pram round the corner and out of sight, then he turned reluctantly as the school bell announced the end of break.

Just before they entered the classroom, Alan whispered, 'We go tomorrow at lunch break. OK?'

'Must we?' groaned Terry.

'You've got to! I dared you! You're not going to let me down are you?' cried Alan.

'Don't be daft!' sighed Terry. 'I'll go.'

They went to their classroom, but Terry could not concentrate on anything. It was not even the thought of carrying out the dare. Terry felt numb, as if partly asleep. For some strange reason he kept thinking about the old man on the bus but he could not think about him in an ordinary thinking way. The image was just there, held in his brain in the same way as a camera holds a picture inside it before it has been developed ... and that night he had a strange dream.

He dreamt he was walking down a very long, red, dusty road. On either side, the hard, heat-cracked landscape stretched away till it disappeared into a wavery heat haze.

Above him, the sun burned, making his head ache and his mouth swell. He could see a farmer in the distance, swinging a spade in slow motion as he hacked at the soil. A solitary

bullock walked round and round a narrow well, hauling a dripping bucket of water which tipped itself into a gulley, and disappeared without trace into the parched earth. It seemed that the bullock must walk in circles forever, and still not bring up enough water for the thirsty crops.

Terry felt thirsty too. He would have crossed the fields to reach the well, but suddenly he saw a gate. Beyond the gate was a bungalow and a large, green, mango tree which cast its shade all round like a pool. Leaning against the trunk of the tree, with his eyes closed, was an old Indian man. It was Terry's old man, sitting cross-legged and deep in thought.

Suddenly his eyes flicked open and looked at Terry. His penetrating gaze seemed to pierce him like an arrow.

'I'm thirsty,' said Terry, opening the gate. But though he walked towards the old man, somehow he never got any nearer to him. The man under the tree seemed to hover just out of reach.

Suddenly the old man got to his feet and came towards him smiling, carrying in his hand a silver pitcher of water.

'Welcome home, Terry,' he said in a strange voice.

'Do I know you?' asked Terry in his dream.

But the old man smiled and drifted away again. 'Just remember we have met,' he said, then Terry woke up with the feeling that he had nearly made an important discovery.

The next day at lunchtime, Terry joined Alan in the cloakrooms where he found his friend dancing with impatience.

'Aren't we going to eat lunch first?' groaned Terry. 'I'm starving!'

'No time,' replied Alan decisively. 'The film starts at one thirty, so we've got to go now. Come on, we'll get something to eat inside the cinema.'

Grabbing their anoraks, they joined the trickle of children who went home for lunch and slipped through the school gates. Once out, even Terry felt carried away by the sense of freedom. He and Alan broke into a jog and did not stop till they reached the underground station.

The ticket hall had been swept clean. Terry and Alan hung about near the barrier watching anxiously for any sign of a dropped ticket. Then Alan saw one, half hidden near the ticket collector's cabin. He wandered over casually, bent down as if to tie his shoe lace, and quickly scooped it up and returned to Terry.

'Got mine!' he announced triumphantly. 'Just got to get yours now. There'll be a train coming in soon, then there's bound to be one.'

Terry nodded, dumbly. He would have given anything not to be doing this dare.

'Can't we give it up, Alan? I've got some money at home. Let's go properly . . .' but Alan didn't hear him. The rumble of a train drowned everything. Soon a small crowd of people flooded up to the barrier, pressing their tickets impatiently upon the ticket collector.

Then one passenger stopped to pay extra. The others pushed past him, dropping their tickets on to the counter. Inevitably, one fluttered to the floor.

'Now,' hissed Alan. 'Get it, quick!' He gave Terry a push.

Terry darted in among the legs, retrieved the ticket, then while the ticket collector was still dealing with the outgoing passengers, the boys marched innocently through the barrier waving their false tickets at him.

'Easy! Isn't it!' boasted Alan, as they stood on the platform. Terry only grunted unenthusiastically. 'Come off it, Terry!' grumbled Alan. 'What's wrong with you? Anyone would think I'd asked you to rob a bank. Going soft, are you?' he taunted, irritated by Terry's mournful face.

A train hurtled into the station, squealed to a halt and opened its doors to them. The boys charged into a compartment, leaping into several seats before they made up their minds where to sit. At last they flopped down, panting; the doors slid shut, and they were off.

Terry sank back with relief. The worst was over. He began to feel elated. There was nothing to worry about. They were sure to slip easily through the barrier at Leicester Square. It was always so crowded.

As the train sped through the black tunnel, the boys amused themselves by making faces at each other in the reflection of the windows.

At last they reached Leicester Square. The doors slid open and Terry and Alan tumbled out on to the platform as another hoard of people elbowed their way in.

The doors slid to an uneasy close, trapping odd parts of coats or skirts, and the train moved off. As it gathered speed, Terry threw one last glance at the people flashing past, and there he was! The old Indian! In that split second he saw him! In that instant, the old man's eyes flew open, fixed on Terry, and then he was gone as the train rushed into the tunnel and was swallowed up.

'Terry! Stop standing and gawping like a zombie! We'll be late. Come on, let's get through the barrier.' Alan dragged Terry into the flow of people streaming up to the escalator.

'Got your ticket?' Terry nodded. 'Good. Now, don't forget. Give the bloke your ticket, and vanish! Walk – don't run – but be sure to dodge out of his sight as soon as you are through. Just melt away! Right?'

Terry nodded wearily. Suddenly he had lost all his enthusiasm again. He felt dead inside. He allowed the force of the crowd to sweep him on to the escalator and stood, unfeeling and uncaring, as he was carried up ... and up ... nearer and nearer to the top.

At the top, the pressure of people behind Terry pushed him off the escalator and relentlessly towards the ticket collector. He could see Alan in front. He had chosen to walk close to a rather fat lady who was fumbling with her shopping basket. As the ticket collector's attention was on her, Alan slipped him his ticket and was through.

Terry lost sight of Alan immediately. Anyway, the collector didn't seem aware that he had just collected a dud ticket and was carrying on collecting the rest.

Terry reached for the ticket inside his pocket and held it out ready. As he approached the barrier he suddenly saw Alan leaning up against a book stall watching him expectantly. He felt the ticket whipped from his fingers, and that was the moment when he should have nipped away into the crowd and done his disappearing act, but there, straight ahead of him, sitting cross-legged in the middle of the ticket hall, with all the world streaming round him as a river flows round a rock, was the old Indian man!

Terry stopped dead in his tracks, gaping in disbelief. 'It's not possible!' he cried. 'I've just seen you going off in the train. It took you away! You can't be here!'

'Oi! You there!' It was the booming voice of the ticket collector. It rang above the noise and rumble of the crowds, turning people's heads; it brought another inspector running.

But Terry could not move. He thought he could hear Alan's voice somewhere calling, 'Run! Run Tel!' But his legs seemed paralysed. He just gazed fascinated at the old cross-legged Indian who almost seemed to be floating

towards him, his black-rolled umbrella hovering in front.

Terry felt a vice-like grip on the back of his neck, and a voice spattered in his ear. 'Come with me, lad. You've got some explaining to do.'

But Terry did not seem to notice the inspector, nor the look of horror on Alan's face. His eyes were held, as if locked by the old Indian's eyes, until he was wrenched away and forced to frogmarch to the station master's office.

'What's your name? Where do you live? How old are you? Have you done this sort of thing before?' Questions, questions, questions! Terry's head was reeling.

After the police had taken down all his answers in a notebook, they began making telephone calls. One to the Social Services, one to Aunty Eileen and one to Police Headquarters. Finally a policeman said, 'Right, lad! We are taking you home now.'

How many times had Terry dreamt of riding in a Police car? Played games, rushing round going 'dee dah ... dee ... dah ... dee ... dah ...' He had even fancied the idea of being a policeman when he grew up. But now, as he sat huddled in a corner of the car with a stern-faced policewoman next to him, he felt no excitement at the crackle of the police radio; no thrill at the sight of the extra gadgets and switches on the dashboard. All he could feel was a bottomless pit inside his stomach, and a dread of having to go back and face everyone at the children's home.

As the police car drew up outside the home, a group of children playing in the garden stopped and gawped. There was a flutter of curtains at the window and Aunty Eileen came down the steps to meet them. The look of disappointment on her face struck Terry to the core.

'Why you, Terry?' she murmured as she came up to them.

Terry rushed inside and up to his room, where he flung himself down on the bed in anguish. Time went by. Terry had no idea how long. The police car went away after a short while, but no one came up to disturb him, not even Paul.

Supper time came, and Terry could hear the clatter of plates and cutlery as the children set the table. Their laughing and chattering made him feel alone and unwanted.

Suddenly he heard a car draw up. Perhaps it was Aunt May. He rushed to the window. No! It was not Aunt May's little white Mini, but the larger, dark red Ford of Mrs. Stevens, his welfare officer! His heart lurched. He heard the front door open and voices in the hall. His name was mentioned, but then the voices were cut off as they went into the living room.

Terry opened his door and stood on the landing, leaning over the bannister trying desperately to hear what was being said. Were they going to send him away? What was going to happen to him? What could he do?

The answer came to him in a flash! Why, he would run away! Without reflecting further, he slipped back into his room and shut the door. Then, grabbing his school bag, he stuffed it with a few clothes from his drawer, emptied his money box, and only paused slightly by his bed to give a last loving look at his pin-up poster of the Manchester United Team.

He had to move fast because once Mrs. Stevens had gone, he would no doubt be called for supper. So, slinging his anorak over his shoulder, he tiptoed out on to the landing again and slid down the bannister on his stomach.

All the children were in the television room now, so he ran quickly across the hall into the kitchen and out of the back door. Leaning up against the wall in the back alley, was his bike. He would definitely take that – it was his most treasured possession.

He did not go to the front of the house where he might be seen, but hurried up the back alleys which ran between the houses until he reached the next road. Then he jumped on his bike and cycled as hard as he could for the park.

He wasn't sure where he was going at first, except that the park was big enough to hide in for the moment while he thought out a plan of action. Keeping away from the main gates, in case he should be spotted by someone he knew, he cycled round the side until he came to a narrow pedestrian way from which there was another entry into the far side of the park.

He began to feel excited. This was going to be a great adventure. It even beat going to the pictures. This part of the park was wilder and more deserted. Lots of bushes lined a rather narrow, grubby river which separated the park from the golf course. If he could get his bike over the river, he could cut across the golf course to the canal on the other side where there were some old warehouses. He could creep in one of those for the night!

Terry cycled in and out of the bushes along the top of the bank, looking for a suitable crossing point. He came to where the bank dipped steeply to a pebbly shore, and where the languid, muddy water had barely the strength to carry away the frailest of twigs. Here it seemed to be shallow enough for him to cycle across, if he could get up enough speed on the slope down into the water.

He stood studying the situation for a moment, then took a deep breath as he thrilled at the prospect of crossing into the forbidden, mysterious landscape of the Golf Course beyond.

Terry stood astride his bike, pointing it headlong down into the shallow river bed, his anorak and bag hung round his neck. Then, with a quiet but jubilant 'Yahoo!' he pedalled furiously and plunged down the slithery bank into the water, sending up a spectacular arc of spray behind him as he zoomed across to the other side. He turned and laughed out loud! He felt brave, but most of all, he felt free!

Terry ran his bike through the long feathery grass towards the trees. It was a late summer evening, and though about seven o'clock, the sun was still hanging in a deep blue sky, clear of the horizon. When he reached the shelter of the wood, he flung himself down in the grass and gazed up at the billowy, white clouds which rolled away in layers like a mountain range.

He felt like a king! The warmth of the sun beamed down on his face, and a sleepy glow spread through his body. Somewhere close by, an invisible cricket chirped and chirped in the long grass; a bee droned its nosey way among the clumps of purple clover, and Terry closed his eyes drowsily.

He surely couldn't have fallen asleep? Yet when Terry next opened his eyes, the sky was no longer blue. Its colour had been drained and now tufts of grey cloud drifted steadily across the heavens like smoke signals, piling themselves up into a dense barrier between sun and earth.

Terry sat up and shivered. A brisk wind eddied through the grass and brought the skin on his arms up in goose pimples. He searched his bag for a jumper, but it had been hot when he left and so he had not thought to pack one. So he pulled on his anorak and zipped it up to his neck.

He stood up and stretched, looking anxiously at the threatening sky. A distant voice yelled faintly from afar, 'Fore!' A golf ball whizzed through the air and thudded at his feet. Terry could see an angry figure poised on the horizon, brandishing his golf club.

Overwhelmed with panic, Terry heaved up his bike and began to run. He skirted round the sandy bunkers, but rode recklessly down the grassy craters and hauled himself up the network of paths on the other side.

Soon he would be on the towpath beside the canal and safe from any accusations of trespassing. Half pushing his bike and half cycling, he at last reached the rough, outer boundaries of the golf course, and saw the muddy track of the towpath running in a straight line ahead of him.

A fine drizzle was falling by the time Terry cycled alongside the canal towards the complex of old, deserted warehouses which he knew were further down. With his head tucked down, Terry barely glanced at the sombre waters, trembling uneasily under the darkening sky, and he did not notice the old Indian sitting cross-legged on the opposite bank; his eyes closed, his up-turned hands resting on his knees and his black rolled umbrella still laid before him, though the rain fell steadily down.

Terry pushed open a broken door, half hanging on its hinges, and stepped inside one of the warehouses. It was very dark and gloomy, and a dank, unpleasant smell hung in the air.

He shivered, realising now how wet he was, with his trousers clinging to his legs, and his hair dripping down his neck.

An hour ago, when the sun had been shining, and he was escaping on his bike, Terry felt like a hero and life seemed exciting. He had felt powerful and independent with the world at his feet. But now, with the cold creeping down his back, wetness seeping into his bones and the realisation that he had not eaten since breakfast, the glory began to fade and he wished more than anything that he was back at the children's home in front of Aunty Eileen's shepherd's pie.

For several minutes, Terry just stood a little way inside the warehouse because he did not know what else to do. The concrete floor was hard and dirty; bits of rag and empty beer cans indicated that other odd wayfarers had found shelter here too, but probably none had stayed longer than they had to; this was no place to set up even a temporary den.

Terry looked slowly round, trying to unfreeze his mind and decide what to do. The first thing was to get warm. He forced himself to walk the full length of the warehouse, carefully looking for something that would serve as a covering.

He found a large cardboard box tossed in a

far corner. Terry pulled out all the clothes he had brought with him and spread them on the bottom to make a bed; then he climbed inside and lay down, drawing his knees almost up to his chin. He laid his head on his bag for a pillow and in a few seconds fell into an exhausted sleep.

While he slept, it stopped raining. Soon a moon appeared, at first pale, then brighter as the last light of day faded and the sky darkened to a blue-black. Its light caught the grey clouds still scattered about the sky; it sparkled on the metal wetness of the warehouses and gleamed on the surface of the canal; it struck the green glowing eyes of a hunting cat, and hung like an eerie spotlight over the old Indian who sat by the water's edge, waiting.

Suddenly, the half-broken door of the warehouse creaked on its one hinge. A small figure stood outside, motionless, as if asleep. He turned towards the towpath and walked with a steady tread until he stopped opposite the Indian seated on the far bank. Then this figure, too, sank down cross-legged, placed his upturned palms over his knees with the thumb and first fingers touching, and lifted his face with closed eyes, up to the old man.

The reflection of the moon drifted between them in the water. Then the old man spoke.

'Terry!' His voice floated across; silvery, high and strangely accented.

Terry opened his eyes, and even through the darkness seemed to meet the hypnotic gaze of the Indian.

'The water which lies between us is both a narrow canal and a vast ocean. The two of us are joined across this water by the same blood flowing in our veins. Nothing can separate us, now that I have found you.

'Several years before you were born, my only son left my house in India against my wishes. He crossed the ocean, cut off his hair and beard, put on western clothes and married a foreigner. He betrayed his religion, disobeyed his father and brought sorrow to his mother. In my fury, I disowned my one and only son. He no longer existed for me, and I shut my heart to grief when I heard that he was dead.

'But now I am old. I can see the end of my days approaching ever nearer. I wept and said, "I have no sons to carry on my family's name." Then my wife and daughters reminded me of you, my son's son! They begged me to find you and bring joy back to the family. Thoughts of you began to fill my brain, night and day, until it seemed that my spirit came on ahead to seek you out. But I am coming soon ... I am coming ...'

'Terry! Terry! Where are you?'

Terry stirred inside his cardboard box, the voice breaking into his dreams. He tried to move, but felt as though he had been welded

rigidly into the uncomfortable position he had lain in all night.

Painfully, he eased his way out, rubbing his stiff neck and cautiously stretching his cramped legs. He limped to the doorway and peered out warily, blinking like an owl in the daylight.

Then he saw Alan, standing on the towpath, looking uncertainly from one warehouse to another. Terry watched him for a few moments before giving himself away, and then he called softly, 'Alan!'

Alan bounded forward delightedly. 'Tel! You crazy idiot! Where have you been? You didn't sleep here all night did you?' he asked incredulously. 'They've been out looking for you everywhere. I thought you might have come here. I think they've called in the police. But why did you go and get yourself caught at Leicester Square, you blithering idiot? You could have got me done too! Why did you just stand there? Why . . . ?'

'Have you got any food?' interrupted Terry, desperately. 'I'm starving.'

'Eh?' gasped Alan, halting his tirade. 'Food? Of course not.'

'Or a drink? I must have a drink. Perhaps I could scoop some out of the canal,' Terry muttered wildly.

'You can't do that,' cried Alan, holding him back. 'I saw a dead cat in there as I was cycling down to find you. Look! I'll nip home and get you something. I'll have to make it sharp – I can't miss school again today. Stay here!'

Alarmed at the state his friend was in, Alan grabbed his bike and cycled off as fast as he could.

'Don't forget the drink!' Terry called out after him. Then he wandered over to the canal and flopped down on the grassy bank. His head felt dizzy and his body weak. He closed his eyes, dozing, while nearly an hour went by, and then there was a shout as Alan reappeared, wobbling down the towpath with a plastic carrier bag hanging over the handle bars.

'Here you are,' said Alan, sliding down next to him. Terry snatched the bag and delved frantically inside. There were some crisps, bread, biscuits and a bottle of coke. He did not know which to eat first. He tore off a mouthful of bread while he wrestled with the bottle top, and then he took a gulp of coke, nearly sending his bread down the wrong way. Alan had to beat him on the back till he had recovered his breath. 'Hey, take it easy, Tel!'

Gradually Terry calmed down and ate his way steadily through everything that Alan had brought.

Then Alan said, 'Look, Terry, I must get off to school. Me Dad'll kill me if I skive off again.'

'Do they know about yesterday, then?' asked Terry.

'Yeh! I had to tell them because of you being missing and all that! But I didn't tell them about this place, honest! What are you going to do?' Alan stood up as he asked the question and got astride his bike.

'I dunno!' replied Terry listlessly. 'I'll think about it.' Then as Alan cycled off down the towpath, he shouted after him, 'I'll go to Aunt May's!'

Aunt May's little white Mini was outside her house as Terry cycled down the road. But when he got to her gate he began to have second thoughts. After all, she was one of them. She would take him back to Julian Road and they might still send him away.

Paralysed by indecision, Terry loitered outside her gate when suddenly the front door flew open, and Aunt May came running down the path.

'Terry! Terry! I'm so glad you came to me. Come in, dear, you must be exhausted. Ever since they told me you were missing I've been waiting, and I even baked your favourite cake.'

She took his bike from him and propped it up inside her gate; then very firmly she clasped his arm and led him into the house.

'I didn't really want to do it ...' faltered Terry, trying to explain. 'It was a double dare ... and ...'

'I know all about it, dear,' said Aunt May, bustling in with a glass of milk and a slice of cake. 'Your friend Alan has told us all about it. He said it was his fault for daring you!'

'Will they send me away?' whispered Terry.

'I doubt it,' said Aunt May, reassuringly. 'What you did was very wrong, but I think they'll give you one more chance. I've just rung Aunt Eileen and told her you're safe, and she told me a relative is trying to get in touch with you. I don't know any details, but Mrs. Stevens has received a letter. So we can't have anything hanging over you now, can we?'

Terry was silent. A thousand thoughts and images seemed to flood through his mind.

'Is my mother a relative?' he asked slowly.

'Yes, but it's not your mother, Terry. It's an Indian relative who wishes to meet you. When you've finished your milk, we'll drive over to Julian Road and hear more about it.'

At the children's home, everyone was seated round the dining table. They always sat at the dining table when there was anything serious to discuss.

In the middle of the table was a large vase of dahlias. Terry kept looking at them, seeing the faces of the adults at different angles through the stalks and flower heads.

At first they talked about his double dare and how this time he would be given one more chance. Terry's mind began to wander as they went on and on about things he did not really understand. Then suddenly, Mrs. Stevens was talking to him sharply.

'Are you listening Terry? This may affect your future.'

She held out a blue letter form with strange stamps on it.

'This letter is from a Mr. Jaswal-Singh. He's your grandfather, your father's father. He's arriving in Britain in just over a week's time. He wishes to see you. Aunt May says that she is willing to take you to Heathrow airport to meet him. Would you like that?'

Terry nodded enthusiastically. He had never been to an airport before. Perhaps he would see Concorde.

'Well then,' exclaimed Mrs. Stevens, 'no more Double Dares!'

The day Terry went with Aunt May to Heathrow was a Double Treat. He had to take a day off school, *and* go to the airport! He and Aunt May stood in the busy arrivals hall, in front of a huge board which looked like a giant calculator.

It clattered and changed from one city of the world to another; numbers of aircraft, times of arrival; whether early, late, delayed or cancelled. They looked and looked, especially at the arrival from Bombay of flight AL 307, due in at 13.30 hours.

It was now two o'clock, and still the plane had not landed. Aunt May began to get restless and walk up and down, but Terry could not take his eyes off the board. At last the word 'landed' flicked up, and he gave a whoop of excitement.

'It's landed, Aunt May! It's landed!'

Aunt May put a hand on Terry's shoulder. He was trembling a little, and she knew that he understood the importance of this moment. For the minute his grandfather walked through the barrier, Terry would never be the same again. He would never be just Terry Singh of Julian Road Children's Home, with no known mother, no father, no family of any kind; the instant he came face to face with his grandfather he would become a grandson, a nephew to his aunts, and a cousin to their children. Suddenly he would find himself part of a great, big family, all his own!

'How will he know us?' asked Terry.

'I'm not too sure,' said Aunt May in a perplexed voice. 'He may have been sent a photograph of you, for his letter was quite confident about recognising you, and he only asked that you should be waiting at the barrier on his arrival.'

Terry and Aunt May threaded their way through the milling throng of saried ladies, excited children and eager families, till they managed to squeeze themselves into a spot right by the rope which stretched from the exit door of the Customs hall to the outside world.

Trickles of passengers were now pushing their luggage trolleys through the flap doors, and with each influx, the waiting crowds surged forwards expectantly, then dropped back.

'How many people can a Jumbo Jet carry?' asked Terry despairingly.

'About three hundred, I think,' sighed Aunt May.

'I think we've seen two hundred and ninety-nine people go through,' groaned Terry.

'It certainly feels like it,' agreed Aunt May.

Suddenly, another surge forward drew their eyes yet again to the swing doors. A group of passengers trouped through; a harassed mother with a wailing baby in her arms, two younger children pushing an over-loaded trolley, looking as if any minute they would all career away out of control; a father with his arms full of suitcases and duty-free carrier bags and, just a little behind, an elderly Indian man, wearing a white turban and an overly-large tweed overcoat, on top of narrow, white, wrinkly pyjamas. In one hand he lightly carried his holdall, and in the other, hanging on his wrist, was a black, rolled-up umbrella.

'There he is!' cried Terry, instantly. 'That's grandfather!'

'Wait a moment, Terry. You could be wrong. How do you know?' asked Aunt May, trying to restrain him. They had seen several elderly Indian gentlemen walk by. Why had Terry recognised this particular one?

Then she knew without any doubt that Terry was right. The elderly Indian looked straight at them, his black eyes glittering like diamonds above his silvery-grey beard, and without any hesitation he glided towards them.

'You are Terry!' he announced in a high, accented voice, without any question mark in his tone.

'But . . . but . . . how on earth did you know each other, just like that?' gasped Aunt May in amazement.

The old Indian put down his holdall and took both Terry's hands in his. 'Terry and I know each other very well, don't we Terry?'

Terry nodded, with a great smile stretching from ear to ear. 'Yes, Grandfather.'

4   Mr. Winterbourne

Down in the basement flat below Maggie lived Mr. Winterbourne. He had lived there for years and years, ever since the war people said.

He had been wounded in the war and was sent home with half a leg missing, but it didn't stop him riding a bicycle, and when Maggie was learning to ride her bike, wobbling along on the pavement, Mr. Winterbourne would cycle past, thrusting one pedal down with his good leg, and using his up-turned wooden crutch on the other. His half leg was always tucked neatly and mysteriously into his trouser leg.

'Go on, Maggie!' he would shout encouragingly. 'It's easy! Look I can do it with no hands and only one leg!'

And he would shoot his arms and wooden crutch up above his head, while Maggie and her bike toppled to a stop, laughing and amazed.

That was a year or two back. Since then, Mr. Winterbourne had become ill.

'After all,' Maggie heard her mother say over the fence to Mrs. Bailey, 'he must be getting on a bit. I can remember him when I was a child.'

He was getting on a bit, though it was easy to forget it, for, apart from his missing leg, he had always been as fit as a fiddle. Cycling had probably kept the rosy shine on his cheeks and the strength in his body. He had been terribly strong.

The children adored him, especially when he swung them about or chased them, roaring like an ogre as he hopped after them with giant hops!

But old age crept steadily on, as it does, and as one generation of children grew up, he didn't swing the younger ones around when they came along. And very gradually, so that people hardly noticed, he didn't cycle quite so much.

Then one day there was an ambulance at his door.

'What's happened?'

'What's the matter with him?' There was a flurry of concern among the neighbours.

'He's had a heart attack,' announced the Polish landlady, Mrs. Popolski, standing on the front steps with her arms folded.

Later, when Mr. Winterbourne came back from hospital, he disappeared into his basement flat like a hedgehog about to hibernate.

'He needs someone to look after him,' sympathised Maggie's mum.

'I could do some shopping for him,' cried Maggie, eager to help.

'He's got someone,' said Mrs. Popolski shortly, almost as if she disapproved. 'His sister's supposed to be coming from Torquay.'

'Well there you go,' said Mrs. Jeffries from the top floor flat. 'All these years and I never knew he had a sister in Torquay.'

'Neither did I,' retorted Mrs. Popolski grimly and went into her own flat, muttering furiously in Polish and slamming the door.

The next announcement caused even more consternation. 'Mr. Winterbourne's taking up painting!'

'Painting?' exclaimed Mr. Jeffries from the top floor flat, as if he'd never heard of it.

'Painting?' shrieked the neighbourhood children, who thought painting was something you only did at school.

'He's taken up painting,' repeated Mrs. Popolski, like a disapproving but adoring mother hen. 'You should see his room! It always used to be a picture of tidiness – but *now* ...'

Maggie knew all about that. She had taken to visiting Mr. Winterbourne most days. At first she used to sit on the stairs and peer into his room through the bannisters.

Since he had taken up painting he began leaving all his doors and windows open, whatever the weather.

'A painter needs light!' he would proclaim grandly.

'And a man needs varmth, Mr. Vinterbourne!' retorted Mrs. Popolski tartly. 'And you vill catch your death vone of these days.'

But Mr. Winterbourne took no notice, and Maggie would sit on the stairs and watch him hunched over a sketch at his kitchen table, whistling through his teeth, among unwashed plates and cups, pots of marmalade and the crumbs of his favourite cream crackers.

At first the neighbourhood children used to hang around as well. They clustered like noisy monkeys outside his window, or dashed in and out of his room trying to catch glimpses of his pictures. But Mr. Winterbourne seemed to paint nothing but bowls of fruit or do endless sketches of bones and hands and feet, so they

soon got bored and stopped coming, and Maggie became his only regular visitor.

'Why do you draw so many skeletons, Mr. Winterbourne?' asked Maggie one day.

Mr. Winterbourne laughed. 'If I'm to be a really good painter, I must begin at the beginning and learn how to draw, just as I would have done if I'd gone to Art College.'

'Why didn't you?' asked Maggie.

'Oh, the war ...' murmured Mr. Winterbourne, vaguely. 'So I'm teaching myself by drawing lots of muscles and bones so that I can paint figures properly, and I do lots of still life.'

He gestured round the room. On every possible surface – the draining board, all along the mantlepiece, on top of the bookcase and propped against the jam jars on the table – were sketches and water colours of jugs, cups, saucers, milk bottles, the kettle, the teapot and even the kitchen sink!

There was nothing he wouldn't draw, and his room seemed almost buried under thousands of sketches and screwed-up drawings which had gone wrong.

'You're getting quite good!' commented Maggie.

'Do you really think so?' asked Mr. Winterbourne, as though her remark really pleased him. 'Why don't you draw too? Here!' And he pushed aside some of the muddle on the kitchen table to make a place for her, and gave her some paper and pencil. 'Go on! Draw that vase on the mantlepiece.'

Maggie, her tongue sticking out between her teeth, carefully began to copy the vase. At first it looked all wrong and she screwed it up in a temper.

'Drawing needs practice like everything else. Anyone can do it if they practise,' said Mr. Winterbourne. So she tried again and again, and after lots of encouragement she finally produced a respectable looking vase.

'I must go and show Mum!' cried Maggie excitedly and dashed upstairs.

Her mother said, 'That's a nice vase!' and Maggie happily propped it up on the television.

Maggie did a drawing every day, and soon their flat was becoming as cluttered as Mr. Winterbourne's.

'You're getting quite good!' said Mr. Winterbourne, as Maggie carefully drew a picture of his armchair in the fireplace.

'Do you really think so?' asked Maggie, and she never felt more pleased.

And then Mr. Winterbourne's sister arrived from Torquay to look after him.

'She's a bit late coming,' grumbled Mrs. Popolski. 'He's well over the worst. Anyway, he manages perfectly well. After all, I'm here!'

When the taxi drew up, the children appeared from nowhere as the word got round, and they all milled about like starlings, staring inquisitively as an immensely large lady heaved herself out of the cab.

The taxi driver dumped her battered suitcase on the pavement and drove off, leaving Mr. Winterbourne's sister standing uncertainly looking up the front steps, while the children sniggered behind their hands. She began to mount the steps.

'Mr. Winterbourne don't live up there!' piped up Johnny Bissell.

'No, he lives down there,' pointed Sheila Macgilvery.

Mr. Winterbourne's sister marched unsmiling down to the basement, completely ignoring the children. Tommy Roberts stuck his tongue out at her, and Maggie decided she wouldn't visit Mr. Winterbourne today.

If Maggie had known Mr. Winterbourne's sister wouldn't last a fortnight, she might not have been so upset. As it was, everything changed the minute she arrived.

From now on his doors remained firmly shut, and net curtains appeared in the windows. Once Maggie caught a glimpse inside Mr. Winterbourne's room. It was completely changed. There was not a sketch to be seen. Everything was washed up, cleaned up, tidied up, and poor Mr. Winterbourne looked fed up.

Maggie tried to keep up her visits, but each time she knocked politely on the door, Mr. Winterbourne's sister opened it, and she always had an excuse not to let her in.

'That child's a pest!' Maggie heard her hiss, as the door was shut on her yet again, and Maggie rushed upstairs, her blood boiling and tears stinging her eyes. She had never hated anyone more than she hated Mr. Winterbourne's sister.

'Things aren't quite the same since Mr. Winterbourne's sister came, are they, Mrs. Popolski?' clucked Mrs. Jeffries. 'Still, he needs someone to look after him, I suppose.'

Mrs. Popolski snorted, 'Look after him? She kill him!' and bursting into a flood of Polish, she stormed into her room.

Then, one summer's morning, just about a fortnight after Mr. Winterbourne's sister arrived and changed things, the whole house was shaken by a terrific disturbance.

It was about eight o'clock, when everyone was either getting ready for school or for work, that they heard first a roar from the basement flat. That was enough to stop anyone in their tracks for a start, but then it was followed by a high-pitched squeal.

Maggie's dad rushed out onto the landing, even though he was only in his under-pants and had shaving cream all over his face.

'What's going on down there!' he bellowed. Mrs. Jeffries leaned over from the top floor with her hair still in curlers, while below, Mrs. Popolski ran out, doing up her dressing-gown, crying, 'Okropne-straszne! Dreadful! Frightful!'

Suddenly there was a resounding crash followed by a tinkle, then such a shouting and banging and crying and clattering as no one had heard since the days when old Charlie Jackstop used to come home roaring drunk.

'Vat shall I do, Mr. Parker?' Mrs. Popolski yelled up to Maggie's dad.

'Call the police! Call the police!' screamed Mrs. Jeffries.

'Don't be silly,' retorted her husband, and dragged his wife back into the flat.

'It's not our business. Mr. Winterbourne is probably sorting out his sister,' said Maggie's dad. 'I say leave him to it!'

'Mrs. Popolski! Mrs. Popolski!' It was Mr.

Winterbourne's voice. 'Call a taxi! My sister is returning to Torquay!'

Mrs. Popolski threw up a look of total joy and scuttled back into her room to do his bidding. 'Yes, Mr. Vinterbourne! Immediately, Mr. Vinterbourne! Thank the Lord!'

So Mr. Winterbourne's sister heaved herself back into a taxi and caught the next train back to Torquay.

By the time Maggie came home from school, Mr. Winterbourne had all his doors and windows open; he had ripped down the net curtains and put out all his sketches and paintings once more.

Maggie stood shyly at his kitchen door, peeping in. She was unable to believe that he was as before, sitting at his kitchen table, already surrounded by unwashed cups and packets of cream crackers, sketching away furiously as if to make up for lost time.

'Hello, Maggie!' he called out cheerily when he saw her. 'Have you come to do a drawing? Come on in, there's plenty of room for you.' And he pushed aside a plate to make some space, and laid before her some paper and pencil.

Maggie glanced round the room and sat down. Everything seemed normal again, except, she noticed that among his usual sketches of street scenes or still life, was a drawing of a face. It was the face of a man looking out with frightened eyes and a worried expression. She stared at it curiously. Mr. Winterbourne didn't usually draw portraits of people though he'd often been asked.

'Who's that man?' she asked, pointing to the sketch, propped against the cocoa tin on top of the shelf.

'Oh, no one really,' shrugged Mr. Winterbourne. 'It's just a face out of my imagination. I saw him in a dream, so I drew him.'

'Yes, he looks like a dream face,' said Maggie, wrinkling up her nose. 'A bad dream!'

Mr. Winterbourne laughed. 'Here! Get on and draw something. How about trying that bowl of fruit there.'

He pushed a dish of apples and oranges in front of her, and placed a banana carefully arched over them. Then he returned to his side of the table.

'I'll get on with my view of Mrs. Dangerfield's bay window across the road.'

They worked side by side for a while in concentrated silence. Then Mr. Winterbourne suddenly stopped. He threw down his pencil and heaved himself up on to his one leg.

Maggie stopped drawing and looked at him curiously, as he stood motionless like a stork.

'I feel ready to go into oils!' he said slowly and deliberately.

'What do you mean?' asked Maggie, who had visions of Mr. Winterbourne pouring a bottle of cooking oil over himself, or rolling on a garage floor getting covered in car oil.

'I feel ready to *paint* in oils, Maggie, and that means I'm getting out my bike tomorrow and cycling to the Art Shop!'

When Mrs. Popolski heard about it, she was quite high-pitched. 'But vhy can't I go for you, Mr. Vinterbourne? The doctor said, "No more cycling!"'

'That was weeks ago, Mrs. Popolski! I feel fit as a fiddle now. Anyway, you wouldn't know what to buy!'

'But vhy can't you tell me?' she persisted.

'Because I don't know myself,' he replied firmly.

So, despite Mrs. Popolski's handwringing and warning clucks, he hauled his bike out from the shed and dragged it up the steps. Leaning on his wooden crutch, he slung his good leg over the saddle, and with a great push, was off!

Wobbling slightly at first, but getting steadier all the time, he rode off determinedly down the road.

* * *

119

'Where's the oil?' asked Maggie, when she called round later to see Mr. Winterbourne's purchases.

'Look Maggie!' he said proudly, pointing to a brand new easel. A spotless canvas stood on it as if waiting to receive his first painting in oil!

On the kitchen table was a large, flat palette, three brushes of different sizes, and about a dozen small white tubes.

'I'll have to starve this month. That lot took all my pension, it did!' said Mr. Winterbourne beaming.

'But where's the oil?' repeated Maggie, looking around for oil cans.

'The oil paints are here in these tubes,' said Mr. Winterbourne excitedly. 'Look!' He picked up a tube marked "Prussian blue".

Maggie leaned forwards intently as he took off the white cap and squeezed the end of the tube like toothpaste. A twist of rich, dark, blue coiled out onto the palette.

'Is that it?' breathed Maggie. 'Watch!' whispered Mr. Winterbourne. He took one of the brand new paint brushes, dipped it into the blue and began to swirl it round on the palette. Then boldly, like someone about to jump into an ice-cold swimming pool, he took a deep breath and dashed a vivid, blue stroke across the canvas!

The paint glowed. It was wonderful. Maggie had never seen such a blue. It made her feel excited. As Mr. Winterbourne swept the brush to and fro across the surface, he almost sang.

'This is why painters love oil! It can be as thick as you like or as thin and pale as you like; you can scrape it, scratch it, shape it or rub it; you can use any tool, not just brushes. You can use a knife or a sponge, or the back of a spoon; you can even ride a bicycle through it – I'll try that one day! Here! You have a go!' he cried, generously handing Maggie the brush.

Maggie, at first shy, and then more daringly, swept the brush across the canvas. She began to twist and twirl the brush, making patterns like the crashing waves of the sea, then she smoothed it out till the blue lay flat and heavy like a late summer sky.

She went into a day-dream and forgot that she was in Mr. Winterbourne's dark, basement flat, where his only view was through the rusty, iron railings to the dull pavements outside. The blue made her think of sandy beaches and seaside; of holiday posters showing Italy or Greece.

'I can see why you like painting in oils, Mr. Winterbourne,' she murmured.

Once more, Mr. Winterbourne was to be

seen out and about on his bicycle, this time with a canvas and easel strapped to his back, and an old army satchel he'd kept all these years dangling from the handlebars with his brushes and tubes.

He went pedalling round the neighbourhood, looking for suitable places to set down his easel. Maggie was always surprised at his choice. He seemed to like finding odd little corners of back streets, or old buildings and terraces – the sort of thing most people wouldn't look at twice, let alone paint. Like the old row of cottages in Brewery Lane, soon to be demolished to make way for a car park, or the derelict church at the bottom of Eaton Road, whose spire used to be the highest thing you could see till they built an office block skyscraper right next to it.

If the weather was wet and he couldn't go out, then he seemed content to paint the view from his basement window in dozens of different ways. Maggie had no idea there was so much to see.

Mr. Winterbourne became famous in a small kind of way. They hung some of his paintings in the local library. The council bought one he did of the Town Hall, and they asked him to do another of the war memorial.

It was the day he went to do his sketches for

the war memorial that Maggie again noticed something odd in Mr. Winterbourne's pictures.

Being a Saturday, she had gone along with him on her bike, with a bag of sandwiches in her saddle bag and her own sketch book in her school satchel.

'This is the view I want of the war memorial,' said Mr. Winterbourne, coming to a stop at the small triangle of green grass. 'If we stay this end, we get the cross in the middle of the picture with the branches of the plane tree in the background. To the left I can draw in a bit of Woolworths, and to the right there is that nice portico into the bank.'

Maggie helped him to set up his easel and collapsible stool. Then when he was comfortably seated in front of his canvas with a box of charcoal to hand, she took herself a little way behind him to the bench and got out her own pad to try and draw the same scene.

They worked quietly and with great concentration for some time, then Maggie wandered over to see how Mr. Winterbourne was getting on.

He had lightly sketched the scene he wanted, and had drawn in the war memorial with quite a lot of detail. But as she stood silently behind him, she saw that he was now working very intently on the figure of a man standing half hidden behind the memorial.

The man looked secretive and strangely sinister. His face stared out, sharply drawn, especially the eyes which seemed to look beyond Mr. Winterbourne, and straight out at Maggie.

'Have you had that dream again, Mr. Winterbourne?' Maggie said at last. 'That's the same face as the sketch back home, isn't it?'

Mr. Winterbourne gave a jump as if he'd been woken from a sleep. 'What did you say? Eh? . . . Everything all right?'

'That man you've just drawn,' repeated Maggie. 'He's got the same face as the one propped against the cocoa tin back home, hasn't he?'

Mr. Winterbourne glanced back at his canvas, then shrugged. 'Has he?' he muttered in a vague sort of way. Then more abruptly he said, 'Come on, let's get going. I've done enough today.'

They packed up their things without speaking and cycled home. By the time Maggie was helping Mr. Winterbourne down the steps with his bike, he was his usual cheery self again.

She carried his bag of brushes into the kitchen and dumped them on the table. Then she caught sight of the new sketches Mr. Winterbourne had been working on. They were the usual scenes he was so fond of – the street outside; the pub near the station and the park gates at closing time, except that somewhere in every picture was the same face, looking worried and frightened.

Sometimes it was a distant face in the background, or with a group of figures in a pub scene, but in others it was right up in front, his eyes looking straight out, watching as if looking for an escape.

'There's that man again,' said Maggie, frowning a little as she felt the unease inside her. 'He's funny. He seems to look at you, like in photographs.'

'Oh it's nothing,' laughed Mr. Winterbourne. 'Those are just doodles. Here, help yourself to a chocolate biscuit!' and he pushed over the biscuit barrel, then put on the kettle for a cup of tea.

But day by day, as Mr. Winterbourne painted and sketched, Maggie could see that something was happening to him and to his paintings. It wasn't just the face, always there staring out at her, it was the scenes he began to paint.

It was as if he was painting two pictures at the same time; the first an ordinary local scene, and then, as if a second hand had taken over, the face would appear, bringing something disturbing, even violent, into the picture.

Maggie watched him paint the house across the road. His sketch on the canvas was detailed and accurate as always, but as he started to mix his oils and add the colour, a terrible transformation took place.

On top of the muted greys and browns of the peaceful street, he suddenly squeezed a vivid orange onto the palette and soon the house on his canvas was on fire, and the staring face appeared in an upstairs window.

One day they cycled over to the canal to paint the bridge and the weekend fishermen. Maggie helped Mr. Winterbourne set out the easel and arrange his palette with the tubes of paint. She was more like an apprentice to him now, helping him to select the colours and squeeze them out onto the palette ready for mixing.

Then she wandered off to find a spot of her own where she got out her pad and began to sketch the bridge, and the afternoon passed peacefully.

Maggie's mother had made them both some

sandwiches, with a flask of tea for Mr. Winterbourne and a can of lemonade for Maggie. After an hour or two, Maggie began to feel peckish.

'Would you like a sandwich and a cup of tea, Mr. Winterbourne?' she asked. Taking the grunt he gave her in reply as meaning "yes", she went over with the bag.

She glanced at his painting and couldn't help giving a cry of alarm. There was the peaceful scene laid out in warm greens and yellows; there was the bridge with the figures of the fishermen taking shape nearby, but also painted in, lying on his stomach in the undergrowth looking straight out at them over the barrel of a gun, was the man, in a soldier's uniform.

His eyes met Maggie's and the gun seemed to be pointing right at her. Suddenly the whole peace of the place was destroyed.

From then on, Maggie began to dread seeing Mr. Winterbourne's paintings. It was as though he was slipping back in time; back to the war forty years ago.

Low, grey aircraft appeared in his skies, hanging threateningly over the neighbourhood; army jeeps mingled with the High Street traffic; tanks exploded on the green and bombs rained through the sky. Houses burned, streets gaped with craters, and soldiers peered through the rubble of shattered buildings.

And each time, somewhere – in a cockpit, behind the wheel of a truck, or glimpsed in a burning window – was the face.

'The war has caught up with Mr. Vinterbourne,' Maggie heard Mrs. Popolski say to her mother. 'I have tried talking to him about it many times. I, too, remember the war. I lost my husband and mother and father in Poland, and I also have many bitter memories. But he will not talk about it so I suppose he must paint it. All these years he has tried to forget; to seal it away. But you cannot do that. It has to come out.'

'It's a good thing we're going on holiday, I reckon,' said Maggie's mother. 'His pictures are beginning to upset Maggie.'

A day or two later, bundled up in the front of a van Dad had borrowed from a mate at work, the Parker family went down to the coast for a couple of weeks.

Maggie took along her sketch book. It was like having a friend with her. When she had got tired of playing on the beach or swimming, she would wander up on to the rocks with her pencil and pad and sketch the cliffs and the waves.

'Mr. Winterbourne's turned our Maggie into quite a good little artist,' said her father.

'Yes,' agreed her mother. 'The school are putting one of her paintings into a competition. It would do her the world of good to win something for a change.'

'I just hope old Mr. Winterbourne sorts himself out. I don't want to have to stop Maggie seeing him,' said Dad anxiously.

He grunted and stretched himself out on the warm sand. 'It makes you realise how lucky we are. The war must have been a terrible thing.' He looked up at the sky with the seagulls whirling round. 'Imagine that sky filled from end to end with enemy bombers! No wonder his eyes can't forget it.'

Maggie stared out at the blue expanse of sea, stretching far out into the horizon till it became the sky. She remembered the first excitement when old Mr. Winterbourne had squeezed the tube of paint marked "Prussian blue", and how it had coiled out onto the palette like a vivid piece of sky.

Who was the man in his paintings? If only she knew that perhaps something could be done to help Mr. Winterbourne. As it was, he seemed to be taken over by a ghost from the past who was forcing him to remember the terrible scenes of war.

Maggie sighed and went back to sketching. The holiday was half over, and her pad was quite full. She thought some of her drawings were good, and she looked forward to showing them to Mr. Winterbourne.

The afternoon they returned home, all the neighbourhood children were out and about. They rushed over to the van as it drew up.

'Got anything for us?' they clamoured.

Maggie waved a bag of rock she'd bought and handed it round, keeping one by for Mr. Winterbourne.

She looked down the basement steps to his window and saw that the curtains were drawn.

'Oh no!' she cried. 'Don't tell me Mr. Winterbourne's sister's come back from Torquay!'

'No!' replied Johnny Bissel. 'It's just the old fellow's gone a bit queer in the head! That's what my Mum says.'

'He don't go out no more,' cried Sheila Macgilvery, 'and he's keeping all his doors and windows shut – worse than when his sister was here.'

Mrs. Popolski met them on the stairs as they heaved their cases and carrier bags up to their flat. She looked worried.

'I'm so glad you are back,' she cried, sounding almost tearful. 'Mr. Vinterbourne, he get worse. I say to him, "Let me call doctor!" but

130

he say, "no, no!" and he shut the door on me. I shout at him through the door. "Mr. Vinterbourne, vhy you keep doors and vindows shut now. You say painter needs light!" And you know vhat he reply?' The Parkers shook their heads. 'He reply, "I don't need light any more, Mrs. Popolski. I'm painting the dark!"'

'That's awful!' exclaimed Maggie's mother.

'I'm going to show him the drawings I did on holiday,' cried Maggie. And before anyone could stop her, she had run down to the basement flat with her pad.

The adults shrugged at each other, and Mr. Parker said, 'She might do him some good.'

Maggie knocked on the door. 'Mr. Winterbourne! It's me, Maggie! I'm back from holiday. I filled my sketch book. Would you like to see?'

She heard the one word, "yes", so she tried the door and it opened.

It was so dark in the room that Maggie couldn't see anything distinctly for a while. Mr. Winterbourne sat as usual at the kitchen table but staring at a blank piece of paper. Maggie held out her sketch pad.

'Look, Mr. Winterbourne! I've been sketching the sea and the cliffs. It's a change from Eaton Road, isn't it!'

Slowly he looked at her drawings and began

to turn the pages of the pad. As he did, Maggie looked carefully round his room. Her eyes had adjusted to the gloom now, and she could see that it was crammed with canvasses and sketches, lying higgledy piggledy all around, as if he had painted his pictures then no longer cared about them.

Each picture that Maggie saw was a picture of war, and his colours were dark and despairing, the colour of war. Each picture had the face, sometimes only the face, staring out.

'They're good, Maggie!' His voice broke into her thoughts. 'You're an artist, that's for sure!'

'Perhaps I could go to Art College when I grow up, like you wanted to,' said Maggie.

'Maybe, maybe,' he said, almost sadly, handing back the sketch pad.

'Can I come with you next time you go out painting?' asked Maggie, hopefully.

'Maybe, maybe,' murmured Mr. Winterbourne, and he bent over his blank piece of paper and began to draw.

Maggie quietly said goodbye and went back upstairs.

While her parents were unpacking, Maggie leaned dejectedly out of the window, watching the children playing on the pavements down below.

Suddenly, a figure caught her eye. An old man was standing on the pavement opposite, staring up at the house. For a split second his eye caught hers.

Maggie gave a scream of fright and dropped back from the window.

'What's the matter!' cried her mother, rushing up. 'Goodness! I thought you had fallen out of the window!'

'Mummy, look! Look out of the window at that man. He's got the same face as the man in Mr. Winterbourne's paintings.' She almost pushed her mother to the window.

'I can't see any man!' said her mother.

Maggie squeezed up into the window next to her and looked out. The old man had moved on, shuffling slowly down the road. 'There! Can't you see him!'

'Yes! But I can't see his face, and really, Maggie, don't you start imagining things too. It's ridiculous!'

'But Mum! He did have the same face!' cried Maggie.

'Maggie!' It was her father's angry voice. 'Don't you start playing us up, my girl. You'd best stop seeing Mr. Winterbourne until he's a bit more normal. Do you hear?'

'Yes Dad,' whispered Maggie, 'but Mum . . .' she tried again.

'Maggie!' They both bellowed. 'Go out and play with the others. Go on!'

A day or two later, as Maggie walked with her friends to school, they drew level with an old man shuffling slowly down the road, his head cast down as if watching the pavement for any unevenness.

As they passed him, he raised his head.

Maggie's heart seemed to leap out of her body. It was the same man and he still had the same face. She was sure it was the face in Mr. Winterbourne's paintings.

He nodded and smiled, but Maggie just gaped and ran. The other children trailed after her shouting, 'Hey Maggie! Hang on! What's the hurry!'

'It's the face,' she muttered to herself. 'It *is* the face.'

After school as Maggie played with her friends, she saw him again, standing at a distance watching the house.

'Have you ever seen that old man before?' she asked Sheila Macgilvery.

'I saw him yesterday, and I think the day before, but not before that. Do you know him?'

'No,' said Maggie. But she didn't tell Sheila that she thought his was the face in Mr. Winterbourne's paintings.

She ran into the house. Perhaps if she could persuade Mr. Winterbourne to come out, he might recognise the man. But just as she was leaping down the steps to the basement, Mrs. Popolski saw her.

'Hey, Maggie. Don't disturb Mr. Vinterbourne. He's taken to his bed, and I'm calling the doctor vhether he likes it or not.'

Maggie went back up the steps and stood at the front on the pavement. The old man was still there, standing very still, just looking and looking. Then he seemed to become aware that Maggie was staring at him, and he turned away and began to shuffle slowly down the road.

Maggie was suddenly filled with a pounding excitement. She wanted to rush up and stop him; she wanted to grab him by the arm and take him to Mr. Winterbourne.

She started forward and called out, but he had already turned the corner. She dropped back, now filled with uncertainty. She heard Mrs. Popolski slam the front door – somehow it triggered her into action. She dashed down the road after the old man. This time she mustn't lose him.

She reached the corner and searched for him desperately among the late afternoon shoppers. Then she glimpsed his white head bent towards the pavement as he moved slowly on, keeping near the shop fronts as if for protection.

Maggie stayed a few paces behind. She did not really know what she was doing, or what she could do. When he drew level with the Town Hall he stood at the zebra crossing, waiting for the green man to flash up. Maggie waited too, a little behind, and when the old man was safely across the road, she, too, dashed over before the green man changed to red.

He arrived at the broad flight of stone steps leading up to the entrance of the Town Hall. A banner slung acrosss the top announced An Exhibition of Local Painters' Work.

'Hello, Maggie! What are you doing here?'

Maggie jumped with surprise, and groaned inside to see Mrs. Jeffries.

'Is your Mum with you?' Mrs. Jeffries asked, looking curiously at Maggie out on her own. 'Has she come about the rent?'

'Er ... no ...' stammered Maggie. 'I er ... I've just come to look at the paintings,' she blurted out, her eye catching the banner and giving her an excuse.

'I've been shopping for a birthday present. My niece is ten in a few days. Now you know what girls of her age like. What do you think of this?' And Mrs. Jeffries began fumbling in her shopping bag.

Maggie could have stamped with frustration. She looked wildly round her. The old man had disappeared. Which way could he have gone? She looked up and down the street, but there was no sign of him. Could he have gone into the Town Hall?

'I must go, Mrs. Jeffries. I told Mum I wouldn't be long. I'll come and see your present later.' And, leaving Mrs. Jeffries in mid-air, she sprang up the Town Hall steps.

'Well I never!' snorted Mrs. Jeffries, stuffing the present back in her bag. 'Strange kid, that Maggie.'

Maggie stood in the cool, dark entrance of the Town Hall. A flight of polished, oak stairs rose imposingly before her. To the right and left, gloomy corridors disappeared like burrows into the depth of the building, with serious doors on either side which did not look as though they should be opened.

'Can I help you?' A bespectacled lady was leaning over a counter just above her head.

Maggie felt taken aback. What could she

say? Have you seen an old man like the one in Mr. Winterbourne's paintings? Maggie took a deep breath. She felt she was about to be cleared off.

'I ... er ... I've come to see the paintings,' she said.

'Follow the finger, then,' said the lady primly, and she stayed leaning on her counter watching Maggie suspiciously as she followed a pointing finger sign up the great flight of stairs saying "To the Exhibition."

At the top of the stairs the finger pointed left. It led her to a large, high room which had a glass ceiling like a greenhouse, through which the light came pouring in. The polished, wooden block floor stretched away before her, empty and echoing under her feet.

The walls were hung with paintings on all four sides. Maggie's eyes travelled slowly round until they stopped, riveted, as she met the gaze of the face staring out of a painting by Mr. Winterbourne.

She walked towards it and stood for a long time. If only the painting could speak.

A voice said, 'Do you like painting?'

Maggie turned to find the old man at her side, his face looking down at her.

She looked at his face and then at the painting. 'That's you, isn't it,' she said at last.

'Yes! That's me,' and he sighed a long, quivering sigh.

'Why has Mr. Winterbourne been painting your face? Who are you?' asked Maggie.

'We were together in the war,' replied the old man. 'He saved my life, and lost a leg doing it. I've been looking for him all these years to thank him. He was rushed off to hospital you see, after it happened, and I never even knew his name. It took me months to

139

find out. Finally I tracked him to an address in Torquay.'

'Yes! His sister lives there!' cried Maggie.

'Well, I wrote there but the letters came back marked "gone away" and giving no forwarding address. After that, I admit, I gave up for years, until I began getting these strange dreams – nightmares!

It was him and me, all the time, him and me, back in the war; struggling through the mud and dodging the mines. Then him and me driving into this village one day and our truck getting shot up.

It overturned and I was trapped. He could have got away, but he came back and dragged me clear, and then this shell exploded right by him! He was only a lad! What future would he have with only one leg? The dreams got me so worked up, I was scared to go to sleep. I knew I had to find him, if he's still alive that is . . .'

'He is, he is . . .' interrupted Maggie, breathless with excitement.

'Then I knew I must do something. I still had that address in Torquay. It was a long shot. It hadn't worked thirty years ago, so why should it work now? Still, I decided to go in person this time. It was my only hope.

I arrived at this house, "Sea View" at the top of the town, and knocked on the door.'

'What happened?' cried Maggie.

'This right battle axe opened the door! Cor!' He wiped his brow at the memory.

'Mr. Winterbourne's sister?' gasped Maggie.

'Yeh! How did you know?'

'She came here when Mr. Winterbourne was ill,' explained Maggie, 'but they had a terrible fight and he sent her packing.'

'Cor!' The old soldier whistled admiringly. 'And him with only one leg! Well,' he went on, 'I told Miss Winterbourne that the War Office had given me that address as being the home of Corporal Edward Winterbourne, wounded in France with the loss of a leg.

"I know what the war did to my brother," she said. "What do you want?"

Then I asked her why she'd sent my letters back marked "gone away" if he had lived there all the time.

"He hasn't," she said. "He went away years ago and never told me, his own sister, where he was going. I didn't know if he was alive or dead till I got a message from the hospital – me being his next-of-kin – telling me of his heart attack. Then I got to know where he lived. I'd have looked after him, even though we never got on – blood's thicker than water – but oh no! He had to be independent, the more so with only one leg ... Anyway," she said, "what's it to you?"

I told her that's what I'd come about. That he'd lost his leg because of me! Then she stared and stared at me. If looks could kill, I'd be dead, sure as eggs is eggs. Then all of a sudden she said,

"I know you! Your face! I've seen your face in Eddie's flat. He drew you over and over again. Drove me bonkers when I told him to stop it, so he threw me out."

That proved it! She gave me his address and slammed the door.'

'But now that you've found him, why haven't you been to see him properly?' asked Maggie, puzzled.

'I meant to but, well, I suddenly lost courage after all these years, and then seeing my face like this in his pictures, it's like seeing my own ghost ...' The old man sighed heavily.

'Is that your daughter, Sir?' It was the bespectacled lady from the counter downstairs, and with her was Mr. Parker.

'It most certainly is,' said Maggie's father. He strode forwards angrily.

'How dare you go off like that without telling anyone. Your mother's been looking for you everywhere. If it hadn't been for Mrs. Jeffries ...'

He stopped dead in his tracks and stared in astonishment at the old man with Maggie. 'It's you!' he gasped weakly. 'We thought she was seeing things; having us on!'

'Will you come back with us and see Mr. Winterbourne?' asked Maggie gently.

'Yes, I'll come,' said the old man, and began to shuffle slowly towards the door.

So at last peace came to Mr. Winterbourne. Maggie took the old soldier to him, the man whose face had haunted him day and night, and gradually the war died away inside him.

His skies cleared of falling bombs; his destroyed buildings rebuilt themselves; once more he saw the quiet suburbs where the children played safely outside, and where the only sirens to be heard were from the factories, signalling the lunch break or the end of a shift.

Nearly everyday the two old men sat at Mr. Winterbourne's kitchen table, talking and remembering the past. Mrs. Popolski brought them cups of tea or joined them in a game of cards, while Maggie often came and sat in the window doing a sketch.

She wondered if Mr. Winterbourne would ever paint again. His easel stood abandoned in the corner of the room, with a blank canvas on it, and the brushes and tubes stayed packed away in his old army satchel.

Then, one morning, when she was out playing with her friends, Maggie heard such a clattering and grunting that she ran in alarm to the basement steps.

Heaving himself out on to the pavement was Mr. Winterbourne and his bike. On his back he had once more strapped the easel, and the old army satchel dangled from the handlebars.

'Hey, Maggie!' he shouted, 'I'm off painting! Do you want to come?'

In a flash Mrs. Popolski appeared on the front steps with her arms folded. 'And vhere do you think you are going, Mr. Vinterbourne?' she demanded. 'You remember vhat the doctor say? He say get rid of that bike. Get a vheel chair!'

'Over my dead body, Mrs. Popolski!' bellowed Mr. Winterbourne. 'Come on, Maggie! Got your drawing things?'

'I'm coming!' cried Maggie, joyfully. 'Just hang on while I dash up and get them,' and she leapt up the stairs two at a time yelling, 'Mum! I'm just off painting with Mr. Winterbourne!'